THE DESERT

Scorching sands and killer Apaches kept most men away.

But not Dave Harmon. He set out across the burning desert with a wagon train, freighting army rifles for Fort Whipple.

Halfway across, his wagons were ambushed, blocked off from water.

They killed one of his teamsters and wounded another. The rifles looked like loot for the killers, and there was a woman along!

Luke Short

Desert
Crossing

DESERT CROSSING
A Bantam Book / November 1961
2nd printing .. November 1962   3rd printing ...... January 1965
New Bantam edition / April 1976
2nd printing .... July 1980

ISBN 0-553-13760-3

Published simultaneously in the United States and Canada

Bantam Books are published by Bantam Books, Inc. Its trademark, consisting of the words "Bantam Books" and the por-
trayal of a bantam, is Registered in U.S. Patent and Trademark
Office and in other countries. Marca Registrada. Bantam
Books, Inc., 666 Fifth Avenue, New York, New York 10019.

PRINTED IN U.S.A.

11 10 9 8 7 6 5 4 3 2

1

The three-masted schooner *Sprite* lay in the Gulf of California just out of reach of the great tidal bore that surged into the wide mouth of the Colorado River. Lashed to either side of her was a flat-bottomed stern-wheeler that was accepting cargo on this inferno of a June day. One of the steamers, the *Cocopah*, was loading goods destined for the river port of Ehrenburg some three hundred miles up the river. The steamboat *Cavalier*, on the other side, was receiving cargo for Yuma.

The last items of the *Cocopah's* cargo were thirty crates of army rifles, one hundred fifty in all, consigned to Fort Whipple, Arizona, and they were stowed carelessly on the steamer's foredeck. Two passengers, a man and a woman, were unloaded by bosun's chair, and the *Cocopah's* crew cast off frantically to take advantage of the favorable tide.

On the journey upriver, when the *Cocopah* was tied up at night to the shore to avoid grounding on unseen sand bars and through days of blasting heat, the rifles remained unnoticed on the foredeck. As the days went by and the *Cocopah* plodded on upriver past Yuma and Eureka, the heat melted the grease the guns were packed with, until oil puddled the deck and threatened other cargo. The crew turned the cases over, but they remained on the foredeck until the day the *Cocopah* slipped alongside the dock of the small port town of Ehrenburg.

Awaiting the boat was a crowd of Mexican, Indian, and white stevedores who swarmed over the steamboat and began unloading the cargo. They slipped on the oil leaking from the rifle cases and, to get this hazard out of the way, the rifles were almost the first cargo discharged. The crew unloading the rifles paused long

1

enough to let the man and the woman down the gang-plank, and inevitably the woman's skirts were stained with the oil her shoes had picked up.

After them came the stocky, grizzled master of the *Cocopah*, Captain Simons by name, with the cargo manifest in his hand; he shoved through the stevedores swarming up the gangplank and headed for a big man lounging against a newly unloaded barrel of flour.

Of the fifty-odd fiercely sweating men on the dock, Dave Harmon was easily the tallest. His height not only set him apart, but so did the black eyepatch he wore over his left eye. Perspiration coursed his sunken cheeks in rivulets, some of it clinging to the full black mustaches over his wide mouth. Perhaps thirty-five, he was a black-browed, big-framed, work-hardened man in stained and careless cotton shirt and wide-brimmed sweat-stained hat. Set deep under his brow, his visible eye was as blue as the summer ocean.

Harmon and Captain Simons shook hands warm-ly, and Dave asked, "Have a good trip, Cap?"

Before answering, the captain turned and looked at the rolling, muddy Colorado River with a practiced eye. Here the river was several hundred yards wide, swollen by the runoff from the high mountains almost a thousand miles away.

"Too early to tell if it's a good trip, Dave. If this high water holds up until I can get up to Hardieville, it'll be a good one."

"You'll have a lot more freeboard after you've un-loaded here."

Captain Simons nodded grimly. "Don't think I'm not counting on that. Just hurry up the unloading, will you?"

Harmon said soberly, "Why, Captain, I was count-ing on you spending a week with me and resting up."

A look of amazement crossed the captain's face, then Dave was unable to keep from smiling. Captain Simons smiled too.

"For a second there I believed you," the captain said. "Lord knows, I'd like to lay over, but if I do I'll be winching this scow off sand bars for the rest of the summer."

Dave grinned. "You'll be doing it later in the summer anyway, Cap. You always do."

"Don't I, though?" the captain said good-naturedly. He extended the papers. "Here's your manifest, Dave."

Dave accepted the papers and started to leaf through them. Turning back to the boat, the captain said, "See you later."

Without looking up, Harmon gestured good-bye and turned and moved warily through the toiling dock workers. Already the dock and the ground beyond were beginning to fill up with sacks, barrels, crates, casks, and kegs. Beyond them lay freight wagons of all sizes and descriptions which were beginning to be loaded in the hot afternoon. Those who had come to watch or to wait for their freight squatted in the shade of the big wagons, and as Harmon moved among them, toward the rear of the big adobe warehouse with attached corral, he greeted an occasional man. Today, he knew, marked the beginning of this summer's labor. The *Cocopah* was the first steamboat to reach Ehrenburg with supplies for the whole central Arizona Territory. There would be other steamers through the summer, of course, but by that time the freighters' wagons would be out scattering this cargo.

Harmon passed the big pole corral which, when full, held one hundred and fifty mules and horses. Now there was only a scattering of animals, for a number of the Harmon Freight Company wagons were down at the *Cocopah*. Dave entered the wide doorway, wide enough to accommodate his biggest wagon, and was immediately in the cooler darkness of the warehouse. Through the far front door he could see the jammed foot, horse, and wagon traffic of Ehrenburg's main thoroughfare.

He tramped down the wide aisle between sparse merchandise, and entered a small cubbyhole that constituted the office of the Harmon Freight Company. Inside was a man standing in the street doorway, a lighted cheroot in his mouth. Dave immediately tagged him as a townsman and the stranger off the *Cocopah*. At the sound of Dave's footsteps the man turned.

"I'm looking for Mister Harmon."

"You've found him," Dave said pleasantly.

The stranger was a stocky man wearing a townsman's linen suit and his full face was newly sunburned. His light Panama hat and the suit somehow hinted of Mexico, but his accent, Dave noted, was probably Mide Western. The few words he had spoken to Dave had an air of condescending authority, and his pale eyes held a half-concealed insolence. He might have been thirty-two, and the rounded belly under his coat suggested that he was used to good living. The breast pocket of his jacket was stuffed with cheroots, and now he changed the cheroot he was smoking from his right hand to his left.

"Somehow I expected a businessman at the head of a freight company."

Dave said drily, "I admit to being one. Maybe my clothes fooled you."

The stranger extended his hand. "Name's Thornton, John Thornton. If the name doesn't mean anything to you now, it will pretty soon."

Dave accepted his hand, which was soft and moist. "How's that, Mister Thornton?"

"I'm a partner in the company that's just bought out the sutler's store at Fort Whipple. I'll be running it and you'll be supplying it."

"I always have," Dave agreed. "Pleasure to meet you."

"There must be a lot of goods consigned to Edwards that came up on the steamer along with me."

Dave only nodded.

"When do you think you can get loaded so we can move out of here?"

"The *Cavalier's* downstream, I hear. It has cargo for Whipple. Edwards' goods will be mixed in with both cargos."

"Two or three days, then?"

"I'd judge so."

Thornton scowled. "Well, do everything you can to hurry it up, will you? I'm in a hurry to get to Whipple." He took off his hat as he drew out a large handkerchief from his breast pocket, then blotted the perspiration from his forehead. "Is it always this confounded hot?"

"Mostly."

Dave started toward his desk when he heard footsteps behind him. He turned to regard a squat, roughly dressed man of fifty, Becket Harney by name, who alternated as head teamster and office man in Dave's absence.

"Where you want those army rifles, Dave?"

"With the Fort Whipple stuff, Beck. Keep 'em separate. Did the lieutenant say anything about posting guards?"

"They'll be here when we lock up, the lieutenant said." Harney nodded curtly and went out into the warehouse.

Turning, Harmon saw Thornton eying him curiously.

"Army guns?" Thornton asked.

Dave nodded. "I'm a contract freighter for the Army, too, Mister Thornton. You're lucky I am. Guns mean a military escort."

"Indians?"

Harmon nodded again. "If it weren't for those guns the Army'd likely hold you here for a week, until they got enough people and goods headed for Whipple to warrant an escort. As it is, you'll be leaving in a couple of days."

Thornton smiled pleasantly. "Then I *am* glad you're under Army contract, Harmon. A week here and I'd be melted down. I don't think the lady could stand it either."

Harmon's heavy eyebrows lifted. "Your wife, Mister Thornton?"

"Oh, no, no. The daughter of Major Frost at Whipple. We came up on the *Sprite* and *Cocopah* from Panama together."

Harmon nodded, his face impassive. "The lieutenant of the detail will tell you the leaving day."

Thornton nodded, said "Good-bye, sir," and stepped out into Ehrenburg's main street.

A woman, Dave thought wryly. This would complicate traveling and camping. Well, she was no affair of his. The Army could look after her, since she was one of their own.

It was long after dark when Becket Harney stepped into the lamp-lit office where Dave was sorting out the shipping tallies for his share of the *Cocopah's* cargo. Harney locked the door into the warehouse and tossed the keys on the desk, saying, "Back doors are locked."

Dave looked up. "Guards posted?"

"Two in front, two in back." Becket slacked into a barrel chair and sighed. "Unless we get some wagons rolling tomorrow, Dave, we're out of space."

Dave leaned back in his chair. "Stack the stuff outside, Beck. With the soldiers on guard it ought to be safe."

Becket shrugged. "Soldiers go when the guns go, don't they?"

At Dave's nod, Becket said, "Why don't we see if old man Sais will rent us that empty store next door?"

Dave shook his head. "Not worth the trouble, Beck. In two-three days we'll have moved enough stuff so we have room. Then this won't happen again until next spring."

"Reckon you're right," Beck said, and stood up. "I figure to get me five fast drinks and some supper. You eaten?"

At Dave's nod, Beck said, "See you tomorrow," and stepped through the open street door. Dave, suddenly bored by his paper work, moved over to the door and looked out.

Ehrenburg, ordinarily a sleepy adobe hamlet of five hundred persons, was stirring with activity tonight. The arrival of the two steamers had brought in men and wagons from the remaining mining camps of La Paz; it had also brought in Mohave Indians from the north who were looking for stevedore work. The wide road before him could no more have been called a street than Ehrenburg, a scattered collection of adobe buildings, could be called a town. Freight wagons, riders, tall Mohave Indians, Mexicans, and immigrants milled aimlessly in the evening. Some of the immigrants were lined up at the ferry landing downstreet, waiting to be crossed over in the night, and some of their lanterns were already lighted. The only other lights in the wide dusty street came from the lamps in stores and saloons that faced the river.

Before he turned back to his desk, Dave noted the two slovenly dressed troopers in idle conversation before the runway door. Back at his desk, Dave stubbornly began to check his invoices against the cargo manifests. He was presently aware of a steady muffled pounding that he idly tried to identify and could not. Returning to his work, he was still aware of the noise. He rose and moved to the street door, and the sound seemed muted. Frowning, he moved back into the room, his head cocked, listening. Slowly then he went over to the runway door which Beck had locked, and put his ear to the panel. Now the sound was more distinct, seeming to come from inside the warehouse.

Swiftly, Dave went over to the desk, picked up the key, and blew the lamp. Returning to the runway door, he drew his gun, quietly opened the door, and stepped into the utter darkness of the warehouse. Now the sound of the rhythmic pounding was more distinct and he moved slowly down the runway, its soft dust muffling his tread.

As he made his way stealthily down the runway, the noise seemed to increase in volume and acquire a different rhythm. There was another thudding sound, softer, that sometimes merged with the first and sometimes played a counterpoint. Moving closer, Dave heard the spill of dirt, and it came to him suddenly that someone was digging through the adobe wall. He moved quietly around the pile of trade goods destined for Fort Whipple and then, so close that he might have touched the speaker, a voice said in a faint whisper, "Take over."

Dave halted as the heavier noise ceased. The dimmer pounding went on. It came to Dave now that there were two men inside the warehouse tunneling through the warehouse wall; because the dimmer noise, hardly more than a jolt felt through the soles of his boots, continued. It occurred to him then that someone was working on the opposite side of this wall, which was a com-

mon one between Sais' abandoned store and the warehouse.

Dave now calculated his chances. If he struck a
match and confronted these two men who had doubtless hidden in the warehouse while his teamsters were
unloading freight from the *Cocopah,* he would have
only the burning light of a match in which to disarm
them. Once the match died, they would either rush him
or break for the door, or hide among the goods in the
jammed warehouse. It would be better, he knew, to retreat, alerting the troopers, and then investigate the
man on the other side of the wall.

Softly now he backed, turned, and quietly made
his way to the office door. The steady sound of the
crowbar, which had led him to the men, was resumed.
Slipping into the office, he went through it and emerged
on the street, where he walked up to the two troopers, whose talk ceased at his approach.

"There are at least two thieves in the warehouse,"
Dave said quietly, tilting his head toward the door.
"They're tunneling through the wall into that old store."
He pointed toward Sais'. "One of you guard the office
door. That's the only way out. The other come with
me."

The two troopers, one young, the other middle-
aged, looked at each other. The older one, with an old
soldier's sure knowledge that survival lay in numbers,
said to the younger, "You watch the office door, Toby.
I'll go with him."

Dave promptly crossed him up. "Go round to the
back of that empty building, soldier, and pick up the
other two guards. I'll take the front."

The younger trooper moved off to take up his
post alongside the office door and Dave gave the older
trooper time to circle the building. Then, moving warily, he walked over to the front door of the building.
What had been a window was boarded up, and he
moved past it, halting at the door. Passers-by jostled
him as he felt for the latch, found it, then hesitated.

He lifted the latch and leaned gently against the
door. The latch cleared its catch and then the movement of the door stopped. Someone inside, he knew,

had propped something against the door to keep it closed. Backing off, Dave ran for the door, the point of his shoulder leading. He hit it with a jolting impact that wrenched the door off its leather hinges. Tripping over the sill, Dave sprawled headlong into the dirt of the floor, and the door came pinwheeling back on top of him.

A gun flash blossomed to his right and Dave snapped a shot at it. He heard the sound of running feet on dirt, and then the back door was wrenched open. Two gun flashes from outside the rear of the store briefly silhouetted a man in the door. Dave heard him fall with a grunt. Now Dave shouldered the door off his back and ran blindly the length of the room. Nearing the rear door he called, "All right, troopers."

Then, suddenly remembering the lone trooper by the office door, he wheeled and ran for the street. He had almost achieved the door when he heard a single rifle shot, succeeded by two swift revolver shots. When he reached the street he saw the pedestrians and riders scattering. The young trooper was standing over the figure lying just outside the office door.

"You all right, soldier?" Dave called.

"Yes, sir. Here's one."

Dave turned and went back through the room. Already the three troopers at the rear had lighted a match, and as Dave came up to them they all looked at the downed man. Dave regarded him curiously; he was lying on his back with dark eyes staring sightless at the ceiling. Blood covered his shirt front, and Dave knew he had died instantly. The man was shabbily dressed in worn and filthy range clothes. From his dark features and black hair Dave guessed he was a half-breed Mohave.

"Anybody know him?" Dave asked.

All three troopers shook their heads.

Dave turned back into the store, heading for the wall where the men had been burrowing. Striking a match alight on the wall, he looked down at the mound of crumbled adobe which had been shoveled aside. Halfway through the hole was a crate, and as Dave knelt and began to move the dust off the crate with his hand, there was slowly revealed the painted legend "U. S. Army."

From behind him one of the troopers said disgustedly, "A whole warehouse with liquor to steal and he takes a crate of rifles."

"Could be what he wanted most," Dave said quietly.

Early next morning Dave tramped down Ehrenburg's only street, heading for a long low adobe building that was the town's only hotel. Ehrenburg was a near womanless town, and somehow its main street reflected it, Dave thought. The biggest buildings were the commission houses which stored and sold goods destined for the stores and trading posts of central Arizona. They were of adobe, as were the saloons, stores, and rooming houses. Because land had little value here, houses and stores were separated from each other, with occasional cottonwoods scattered among the buildings.

The Ehrenburg House was a sprawling, one-story, adobe building located between two of the commission houses and facing the broad Colorado close to the ferry slip. The portion of the building at the left of the entrance held a small bar; to the right was the dining room, and beyond it the bedrooms. Mostly the hotel was patronized by passengers from the steamers and from the California-Arizona Stage Line who wanted a comfortable place to lay over before resuming their journeys east or west.

Dave entered the small lobby, which was deserted. He went across it and looked into the dining room, where he saw Lieutenant Overman, John Thornton, and a girl seated at one of the tables. A pair of drummers at a side table were the only other customers.

Catching sight of Dave, Lieutenant Overman beckoned him over and rose. Overman was a young, slim, fair-haired second lieutenant. His pale mustaches were full, and when he moved he did so with a kind of jaunty laziness. When Dave halted by the table with his hat tucked under his arm, Overman extended his hand. "Morning, Harmon." They shook hands, and then Overman said, "Miss Frost, may I present Dave

Harmon?" To Dave he said, "Miss Frost is heading for
Whipple to join her father, Major Frost."

Dave bowed briefly, military fashion, and Juliana
Frost nodded and smiled. She might have been twenty-
two, Dave judged, but she had the poise of a much
more mature person. He guessed that she was not tall;
her light summer dress of pale blue was in striking con-
trast to her deep brown-black, wide-set eyes. Her pale
hair was gathered at the nape of her neck, schoolgirl
fashion, by a bow of the same material as her dress,
and Dave noticed that the golden tan she had acquired
on shipboard had brought a faint sprinkling of freckles
across the bridge of her straight nose. Her smile, at their
introduction, had been open and cordial.

"You're up and about early, Harmon," Thornton
said. He was dressed in the same townsman's clothes of
yesterday.

"I'm on a recruiting mission," Dave replied.

The lieutenant looked puzzled, then gestured to a
chair. "Sit down and tell us about it."

Dave sank to the chair, aware that Juliana Frost
was regarding his eyepatch. He was used to people accepting his eyepatch in two ways, either with polite re-
vulsion plus curiosity, or with sympathy and over-po-
liteness. He preferred the former. However, there was a
expression of real curiosity in the girl's eyes now, as
she spoke.

"Harmon—you couldn't be the Lieutenant Dave
Harmon who served under my father?"

Dave nodded. "Yes, with Reno. I knew your father
well, Frost. I think you were in school in the East
when I was with him." He paused. "I understand you're
going with our wagons to Whipple."

The girl looked inquiringly at Lieutenant Overman, who said, "Harmon's a contract freighter for the
Army, Miss Juliana." Then to Dave, "Will you be going?"

"It looks that way. It's the busiest time of the year
and that always finds us shorthanded."

Juliana smiled. "Maybe you'll be able to tell me
the truth about Papa's tall stories."

"I wouldn't spoil it for him," Dave said, and smiled in return.

"What's this mysterious recruiting you mentioned?" Overman asked.

"For a burial detail," Dave said. "I assume your men reported to you what happened last night."

Lieutenant Overman nodded as Juliana asked, "What did?"

"Two men were killed by Lieutenant Overman's troopers. They were trying to break into my warehouse."

"Was killing them necessary?" Thornton asked.

"Why, if a man shoots at you, you shoot back," Dave replied easily.

Lieutenant Overman said quietly, "How do you read this, Harmon?"

Dave shrugged. "You can read it two ways, Lieutenant. The two men could have been some of the scum that's always floating around this town. They'll steal anything that isn't nailed down. Maybe a case of rifles was the first thing they happened to lay hands on." He paused. "Or you can read it this way—that the rifles were really what they wanted."

Thornton said, "My guess would be the first. They saw a clever way to loot your warehouse. After all, it's full of everything from trade goods to whiskey, isn't it?" At Dave's nod, he continued, "Besides, a case of rifles is just as salable as a barrel of sugar."

"But what if they were specifically after the rifles all the time? If they couldn't take them from a warehouse, they might make a try on the road," Dave suggested.

"Let 'em try," Overman said grimly. "That's what we have soldiers for."

"How big an escort will there be?" Dave asked quietly.

Lieutenant Overman flushed a little. "Seven men, including myself. With your freighters, Thornton, and yourself, that represents some firepower."

Dave stood up. "If they're good men, it does."

Lieutenant Overman rose too. "We didn't come all the way from Fort Mohave to be bluffed by this mining riffraff," he said grimly. "You'll get your burial detail, Harmon. When do you think we can leave for Prescott?"

"Day after tomorrow morning. Early." Now he turned to Juliana. "I hope you have a wide hat, Miss Frost."

"We have a covered ambulance for her and Mister Thornton. I don't reckon they'll get too sunburned," Overman said.

At that moment the girl came in with a tray holding their breakfast of melon, toast, steaks, and coffee.

"Stay for breakfast, Harmon?"

"I've had mine, thanks." He bowed again to Juliana, turned, and walked out.

Lieutenant Overman waited until the girl had distributed their plates and left, then he said, "If you'll both excuse me for a few minutes, I'll attend to the burial detail."

The ferry on the California shore of the big river, opposite Ehrenburg, was loading a spring wagon and team driven by an old man. The ferry, some forty feet long and railed at the sides, was a rope ferry propelled by the current of the river. The ferryman, a dour German of middle age, wearing a ludicrous-looking Mexican straw hat, moved back to the line preparatory to casting off.

The old man called from the wagon seat, "There was a couple of riders behind me, Herman. Reckon they'll want to cross."

The German nodded and, in a matter of minutes, the two riders approached, dismounted and led their horses onto the ferry. Then the German cast off.

Both riders seemed talked out; they chose opposite rails and did not talk with the ferryman or the old man. Nash Kirby, at the upriver rail, was a squat, bearded man with sun-blackened cheekbones and pale gray eyes. He wore sweat-stained range clothes and scuffed half-boots. His companion, Telesfor Roybal, was a Mexican dressed in much the same fashion as Kirby. Both wore guns and both had rifles in their saddle scabbards. Both men were dripping wet with sweat, as were their horses.

When the ferry reached the Arizona shore, the old man drove off, heading for Ehrenburg's main street. Kirby and Roybal mounted, but instead of going into the town, they turned upriver and followed a trail that led through the lush willow and cottonwood growth of the river bottom. Roybal rode in the lead.

A ride of ten minutes in the broiling sun brought them to a motte of tall cottonwoods, and in a clearing in this motte they came to a campsite. It seemed to Kirby to be quite a large camp; according to the count of blanket rolls scattered around the ashes of the dead fire, at least ten men slept here. A ground sheet thrown over a rope stretched between two trees provided a makeshift tent, and it was toward this that Roybal pointed his horse.

Dismounting, the Mexican ducked into the tent and emerged immediately. Following him came a lean, red-headed man of perhaps thirty, who, although just aroused from sleep, was as alert as a cat. He observed Kirby, who had dismounted, and immediately he smiled. He had a raffish and impudent face that was burned a deep red. And now, as he walked toward Kirby, he strapped on the shell belt and holster which he had in his hand when he came out of the tent. He was called, almost inevitably, Brick, and his last name was Noonan.

As he approached Kirby, he spoke. "Well, Kirby, you made good time."

"After hearing Roybal's story, I thought I'd better not miss it." He looked around him. "What the hell are you doing camped in this backbrush?"

Although these two hadn't seen each other for some years, they did not shake hands. The amenities were a matter of indifference to both men. Now Kirby regarded Noonan with some care. Noonan was dressed in an odd combination of Mexican *charro* pants, calico shirt, and highly decorated Mexican boots.

"I'm staying away from the soldiers, Kirby. You can't ever tell when one of the troopers may spot his old sergeant."

Noonan walked over to a canteen hanging from a low cottonwood branch, drank from it, then moved over to offer it to Kirby. He accepted and drank from it too, while Noonan kicked a blanket roll flat and sat down. Roybal, who had been watching this, came over now, took the trailing reins of Kirby's horse and led both horses back into the trees, where a picket line holding two horses was stretched.

Noonan and Kirby seated themselves on the blanket, sitting cross-legged and facing each other.

"I'm surprised you came," Brick said.

"I'm surprised, too," Kirby answered. "I don't like running with a bunch."

"This time we need a bunch," Brick said.

"Let's hear all of it."

"Thirty crates of army rifles, five to a crate," Noonan said. "Across the border they'll bring a hundred dollars apiece."

Kirby wasn't impressed. "That's what the Mex said. Where are they?"

"Harmon's freight yard. They're headed for Fort Whipple."

"Along with a troop of cavalry, I reckon."

Noonan smiled faintly. "I don't reckon, Kirby. They have a detachment from Fort Mohave of six men and one officer. When I join them they'll have seven men and one officer."

Kirby looked puzzled. "When you join them? What do you mean?"

"Remember I was in the Army?" Noonan asked drily.

"What does that prove? So was I."

"But you didn't keep your uniform."

It didn't take Kirby long to catch on. "Deserted, eh?"

Noonan nodded. "That uniform has come in pretty handy. It will this time, too."

Kirby was silent a moment. "Think you can get away with it, Brick? What if they ask you about names? Like who your officers are?"

"This detachment came down from Fort Mohave. I know the names of enough officers in Fort Whipple to get by."

Again Kirby was silent, then he said, "It's a hell of a chance, Brick."

"I've been taking chances all my life. So have you. What I want to know is, can you run this crew if I'm with the wagons?"

"I run a bigger bunch than this, if you remember."

"Then what do you say?" Brick demanded.

Kirby shrugged. "It's up to you, son. Getting caught will be pure hell."

Noonan smiled faintly. "They've got to find me out first."

"Then what do you plan to do?"

"Hit 'em on their way to Whipple. We've got the men to clean 'em out."

"How many?"

"Fifteen, with you."

Kirby nodded judiciously. "How you going to split this, Brick?"

Noonan grinned. "There can't be any split, Kirby, until I deliver the guns."

Kirby eyed him steadily. "You mean thirteen men are trusting you to go into Mexico and come back with the money?"

Noonan's grin was still there. "They'll go with me, Kirby. You, too. If you want your cut."

"And how much is that?"

"I keep five thousand, and the rest is split equally."

Kirby slowly came to his feet and said mildly, "Hell, why did you bother me with that kind of money?" He started toward his horse.

"Wait, Kirby!" Noonan said.

Kirby halted. "You'll get a thousand of my share besides," Noonan said.

Kirby said gently, "I'll get two thousand, Brick."

Noonan flushed and hesitated only a moment. "All right. Now sit down."

Six days out of Camp McDowell and roughly a hundred miles east of Ehrenburg, Lieutenant Joshua Miller led a ten-man mounted detail with supply wagon westward across the Harquahala Plains. He was in pursuit of a band of Apaches who had raided a mine near Mount McDowell, and had killed and mutilated seven miners before heading west. This was Second Lieutenant Miller's first field command.

Lieutenant Miller çame into his command by an odd series of circumstances. He was slight of frame, sandy-haired, bookish by inclination, and perhaps, because of his size, more aggressive and demanding than his fellow officers. The new commanding officer at Camp McDowell was Major North, a Civil War veteran straight from a desk job in Washington. Lieutenant Miller's last post had been the Presidio in San Francisco, where his last assignment had been the writing of his regiment's history. Neither man had ever served in the Indian West.

Camp McDowell, like many of the Western posts in this year, was not only undermanned, but nearly every trooper except the sick and the housekeeping detail was in the field against the rampaging Apaches. Major North, with few officers from which to select, chose Lieutenant Miller to lead this detail. He had thought it likely that it would be a fruitless chase, but to appease the miners, the newspapers of the territory, and the fearful civilians under his protection, he had to make the gesture of pursuing the Apaches. Accordingly again because of the manpower shortage, he was forced to rob the guard house, the commissary, the quartermaster, and the blacksmith's shop of men to make up the detail. Of the ten men, only one was a non-commissioned officer, Corporal Ira Chasen.

In the month that Major North and Lieutenant Miller had been in Camp McDowell they had both acquired an abiding hatred for the Apaches. They had both heard from eyewitnesses of the nauseating atrocities committed by the Apaches, and both burned with a zeal to avenge them. Major North's dislike of the Apaches extended even to the Indian scouts employed at Camp McDowell. He was convinced, against all contrary evidence, that they were devious and treacherous, and that they would gladly lead any detail into an ambush if given the opportunity. Major North, however, did not give them the opportunity, and that was the reason why Lieutenant Miller on this blazing morning was without a scout.

Since there had been no rain and no wind, Lieutenant Miller and his detail had no trouble following the trail of the Apaches, who apparently were so contemptuous of pursuit that they had not even bothered to try to hide their tracks. This fact was noted by Lieutenant Miller, and it so angered him that he was willing to take Major North's orders literally. Those orders were to capture the Apache murderers and, if they did offer to fight, to exterminate them.

Lieutenant Miller estimated that the band of Apaches numbered seven, and so far as he could tell they had no extra horses with them. Since his detail had rations for two weeks and since their horses, in Lieutenant Miller's opinion, were bigger and better fed than the usual Apache pony, it was simply a matter of time before they overtook the Indians. The lieutenant had reasoned that the Apaches would lead him to water because they needed it themselves, and his six-day pursuit had proved the correctness of his reasoning. How they knew where the water was on this seared desert of sand, rock, and mesquite, Lieutenant Miller didn't know, but if he followed their tracks long enough he knew he would come to water.

Because of the flat, treeless desert plain where a man could see twenty miles in any direction, Lieutenant Miller did not bother with flankers. Yesterday at sunset he had seen a plume of dust against the distant blue of the Harquahala Mountains, and he had guessed correctly that he was overtaking the band of Apaches. Accordingly, because there was a moon later and tracking by its light was easy, he had decided on a night march after an hour's rest. By morning he knew that the Apaches had decided on a night march, too, since there had been no sign of a camp and no Apaches.

By midmorning Lieutenant Miller began to worry. They had hit no water during the night and there was precious little left in their canteens. Some of the detail, against orders to go sparingly on the water, had even emptied their canteens. The horses, long without water, were more weary than their riders. However, Lieutenant Miller, secure in his knowledge that the Apaches and their mounts needed water, too, clung stubbornly to the trail of the Indians.

Corporal Chasen was flanking Lieutenant Miller this morning, as he had done for the last five days. He was a burly man, as befitted a blacksmith, with dark brows as thick as mustaches, over eyes of pale gray. A slow, taciturn man, he carried his rank lightly and was liked by both officers and enlisted men. His rank entitled him to ride beside his lieutenant, free of the dust churned up by the horses. In spite of his taciturnity, this morning he seemed eager to talk, mostly about the shape the detail was in. When he asked the prime question, the lieutenant was prepared for it.

"Lieutenant, you reckon we should turn back before we get in any deeper?"

"We're as deep as we can get, Corporal," Miller said flatly. "We're sixteen hours from the last water. I don't think we can make it back."

The corporal said stubbornly, "At least we know where water is back there, Lieutenant. We don't know if there's any ahead."

Now Lieutenant Miller spoke sharply. "We're very sure there's water ahead, Corporal, and that those Apaches are heading for it. When we come across the first foundered Indian pony, I'll turn back, but not before."

They never found a downed Indian pony, but by afternoon they found water in this heat-blasted plain. It wasn't much, and they had to dig for it, just as the Apaches had. But it was there. The process of watering the detail and the men and filling canteens and waterbags was a lengthy one, and Lieutenant Miller decided to camp. Both men and horses needed a rest, and in their present shape they would be worthless if the pursuit was continued. However, a day's rest and food would fix that, and stubborn Lieutenant Miller decided to continue the chase next morning.

This was a shadeless flat and the heat seemed to have weight and substance. The detail, propping up ground sheets and blankets with their carbines to provide shade, tried to sleep and prayed for the sun to hurry and heel over to the west.

In his own small tent Lieutenant Miller, stripped to the waist, wrote out his daily report. Presently he consulted a map which adhered to his sweating hand whenever it was touched In his report Lieutenant Miller was candid enough to state that he did not know where they were, that he had been traveling west and some south and had not once camped at one of the very few wells that were named on the map. He proposed, he wrote, to take up pursuit in the morning unless weather conditions intervened to obliterate the Apache trail. This last made him smile, since there was not a cloud to be seen in the brassy sky in any direction.

That evening when the sun was down the horses were watered again before being put on the picket line. The troopers had managed to scrounge enough mesquite for two small fires, over which they cooked a meager meal of bacon, bread, and coffee. They were a dispirited group, the lieutenant saw, and he knew they were blaming Corporal Chasen for his inability to persuade their officer to abandon the chase. At dark two guards were posted, and again Lieutenant Miller noted the surly but silent reception with which the news was received. He knew that his men, having ridden all night, were exhausted, and that they thought guarding was not only unnecessary but punishing.

Soon after supper the men rolled in their blankets and slept. Lieutenant Miller made the round of camp and saw that the guards were alert, and then retired himself.

It was sometime after midnight when Lieutenant Miller was awakened by the sudden sound of hoofbeats. He boiled out of his tent, pistol in hand, just as a sentry shot. He was in time to see, in the moonlight, his horses vanish into the blackness to the south.

Running to the two guards, a sudden rage touched Lieutenant Miller. Hauling up before the guards, he demanded, "Wilson, what happened?"

"Sir, I was awake and I had passed the picket line a bare minute before."

"And you, Ryan?"

"I'd come around on the north side of the camp, sir, and was heading for the picket line."

"Neither of you saw anybody?"

Both men said no. By this time the camp was roused. Small fires were rekindled and the troopers stood waiting for orders.

Lieutenant Miller knew he should act, but he also knew he was powerless to change anything. He had taken every precaution a commander should. *No, that isn't quite correct,* he conceded to himself. *I should have had a mounted sentry circling the camp.* Still, in spite of his precautions, his detail was now afoot and in unknown country.

Well out of the firelight Lieutenant Miller paced back and forth. He had heard it said, half in jest, that an Apache Indian could steal a horse from a man who was holding its reins. Now he had bitter proof that this was true. Pursuit of his horses, of course, was out of the question. By dawn his horses would be fifteen miles away, and if he set out after them they would gain hourly on his dismounted detail.

His second choice was to retrace the route they had come. He knew, with a dismal certainty, that by doing so he would lose most or all of his command. A man afoot in this wide and oven-hot desert was almost certainly a dead man. What had seemed impossibly long rides between water to mounted troopers would simply be impossible to the unmounted men.

The third alternative he remembered from his map-reading earlier. A stage-and-freight route from Ehrenburg to Prescott lay far to the north of them. Instead of risking his men by following their old back trail or instead of trying to lead them to the freight road, he would keep the detail here where they were certain of water. He would dispatch a couple of his strongest men to the north, carrying all the canteens they could manage, hoping they could intercept a stage to take them to Camp Date Creek or Fort Whipple, where they could obtain horses to rescue his detail.

Only then did the ignominy of his situation become fully apparent. He had allowed the Apaches to pull him into an angry pursuit that was no pursuit at all. They had led him as far from water and food as they wished and then stranded him. It was easier than an attack, infinitely more safe for the Indians, and the end result might easily be death to the whole detail.

Next morning, after a breakfast at dawn, Lieutenant Miller summoned the troopers of the detail to his tent and explained the situation. It was his decision to remain here until help and horses came, he said. Other alternatives—and he named them—were the equivalent of committing suicide.

After a long pause in which the men eyed each other grimly, the lieutenant resumed. "I propose that the strongest men, packing all the water and food they can carry, head north for the stage road within an hour."

"What men, sir?" Trooper Ryan wanted to know.

Lieutenant Miller said icily, "It would be simple justice, Ryan, if you and Wilson were selected. After all, you let the Indians steal our horses."

There was a murmur of assent among the remainder of the detail.

"However," the lieutenant continued, "I will select two men on the basis of their strength."

"What about drawing lots, sir?" a trooper on the fringe of the circle called.

"Aye, what about that, Lieutenant?" another voice called.

Lieutenant Miller answered coldly, "I am thinking of the safety of us all." He looked slowly around the circle of faces. "There are men in this detail who are rotten with disease and have fought whiskey for so long they couldn't make it out of sight of us. Am I right?"

"That's their own business, Lieutenant."

"Nobody knows what's out there," a new voice spoke up. "You may be sending two men to their deaths."

The lieutenant said angrily, "I'm your commanding officer!"

"And a hell of a one you are!" Wilson said brusquely.

"Corporal, arrest that man!" Lieutenant Miller ordered.

"And take him where, sir?" Corporal Chasen asked with open irony. Then he added, "If the Lieutenant will dismiss the men, maybe we can talk, sir."

Miller hesitated, then he snapped, "Dismissed." The group did not break up, but moved away from the tent almost as a body, talking in low tones.

Corporal Chasen said, "I request the Lieutenant's permission to make a suggestion, sir."

"Go ahead, Corporal."

Corporal Chasen continued quietly, "I think the Lieutenant better let them draw lots. They think it's only fair that way."

Miller retorted, "These men are bound by oath to obey orders!"

"Suppose the Lieutenant orders the two youngest and strongest to go?"

"Yes, suppose I do? You think they won't obey, is that it?"

Corporal Chasen's quiet expression did not change as he said, "Oh, they'll obey. They'll walk out of sight, wait until dark, then come back to camp, and shoot you in your sleep. After that we'll draw lots."

A startled look came into Lieutenant Miller's thin face, and he opened his mouth to speak, then closed it.

Corporal Chasen continued, "You see, Lieutenant, in this fix we're all equal."

Lieutenant Miller scowled. "Are you suggesting that I draw a lot, too?"

Corporal Chasen shook his head, "Oh, no, sir. It's your duty to try and save the men, sir."

"But not in the way I choose?"

Corporal Chasen's face reflected an increasing distaste for continuing this argument. He spoke formally. "The Lieutenant gave me permission to make a suggestion. My suggestion is that the Lieutenant call the men together and ask if anyone wishes to volunteer. When they don't, I would allow them to draw lots. They can start tonight, and travel in the cool."

Lieutenant Miller had made his protest; this was not the way the United States Army did things. This was riffraff government, but behind this feeling of conviction were Corporal Chasen's words. *They will wait until dark, then come back to camp and shoot you, then draw lots.* Lieutenant Miller smiled ever so faintly. "Very well, Corporal, call the men together."

That night Troopers Reardon and Adams, the former a sodden alcoholic, the latter not much more than a boy, left camp. Festooned with canteens, they carried all the food and water they could pack.

2

Brick Noonan, in the few days' time alloted him, had studied his man thoroughly. He was aware that the Fort Mohave detail was camped several dozen yards behind the Ehrenburg House. He was also aware that Lieutenant Overman, with the privilege of rank, was staying at the hostelry and he had made a study of the lieutenant's habits.

Like most junior officers, Lieutenant Overman was not averse to a bit of alcohol, especially during the evenings when a man in Ehrenburg had only three diversions—the cheap Indian and Mexican women, gambling, and drink. It had been Noonan's observation that the first two did not appeal to Lieutenant Overman, while the third did. Apparently the lieutenant favored the discreet small bar in the Ehrenburg House where the more prosperous businessmen and mine owners adjourned each evening for a quiet game of cards and even quieter drinking. Accordingly, it was into this small, one-room bar, holding two gambling tables and several easy chairs, that Noonan came that night. He was wearing a well-worn sergeant's uniform over which he had carefully sifted dust.

Stepping into the lamplit, whitewashed room from its street entrance, Brick Noonan saw his man immediately. Overman, glass in hand, was watching the poker game, and Brick smiled inwardly. *You don't gamble on a lieutenant's pay,* he thought. He walked across the room and halted beside Overman's chair. When Overman looked up, Brick gave a respectful, casual salute that startled Overman, who returned it even more casually.

"May I speak to the Lieutenant, sir?"

Overman, the top two buttons of his blouse unbuttoned, rose and moved the eight feet to the bar, on which he leaned.

"What is it, Sergeant?"

"I'm Sergeant Noonan, sir, reporting back to Fort Whipple from leave."

"What can I do for you, Sergeant?"

"Sir, it's like this. I spent my leave with my brother at Dos Palmas. The night before I was to leave I got lucky in a card game and won a horse. He's a good one, sir."

Lieutenant Overman looked puzzled but polite as Noonan continued.

"I sent all my gear on the stage and rode my horse to Ehrenburg. After I crossed on the ferry I went into a bar and met one of your troopers, sir."

"That's very likely," Overman said drily.

Noonan smiled dutifully and continued. "He told me your detail was headed for Whipple. I'd like your permission to join the detail, sir."

"When's your leave up, Sergeant?"

"I've got a week of it left, sir."

Lieutenant Overman straightened up and smiled. "You're more than welcome, Sergeant Noonan. There aren't too many of us and we could use an extra rifle."

Noonan smiled. "And I could use company, sir. One man isn't much against a bunch of murdering Apaches."

Overman nodded. "You've got your papers?"

Noonan shook his head. "No, sir. They're with my gear on the stage. I didn't figure I'd be as lucky as this or I'd have carried them."

Lieutenant Overman smiled. "Well, Sergeant, if you were intending to desert, you wouldn't be going back to Whipple."

Noonan grinned. "No, sir. I'd be going the other way."

Lieutenant Overman handed his glass to the bartender. "We're leaving at dawn tomorrow, Sergeant. We assemble at Harmon's warehouse. Your horse in good shape?"

"The best kind of shape, sir. Thank you. And I'll be on hand when your detail is." He came to attention, saluted, and walked out.

Lieutenant Overman returned to watch the card game, regarding himself as a lucky man.

Later that night, back in the cottonwood motte Sergeant Noonan rode up to a fire around which ten of his men were gathered. He could see the other two men guarding the remuda. There were other fires within sight, the fires of broke miners who had been thrown out of work by the gradual closing of the placer mines of La Paz, five miles to the north. They were too poor to live in the cheap boarding houses of Ehrenburg, or to travel. They were hungry, desperate, and reckless, and would willingly steal an unguarded horse. Indeed, half of the ten men lounging around the fire had been carefully recruited by Noonan from these ranks.

Kirby was lounging on his blankets, the farthest from the fire, taking no part in the conversation. As befitted the man who would lead this riffraff, he purposely remained aloof. After Noonan had unsaddled, and turned his horse into the rope corral, he went across to Kirby.

"How'd it go, Brick?"

Noonan sat down. "Just like I knew it would." He could not entirely keep the smugness out of his voice. "No questions asked, except about my leave papers. I reckon he was glad to see me."

"You carry your luck with you, don't you?" Kirby said admiringly. "All right, what do you want us to do?"

"Better start moving the men out in an hour or so. I want you to be well ahead of us."

"Where's the first water?" Kirby asked.

"A place called Tyson Wells. Tell your bunch to get water there, then scatter out of sight till dark."

"We ain't got much grub, Brick."

"We won't need much grub if this works, Kirby. If it doesn't, you couldn't pack enough grub." He started to rise, and then as an afterthought said, "Be careful of that woman, Kirby, and also be damned careful of me. I'm the only man with sergeant stripes. Remember that."

It was bare daylight when the seventh loaded wagon pulled out from Dave's wagon yard and joined the six others strung out in a line down the street. They were big wagons, high-sided, with rear wheels as tall as a man, and to most of the wagons were hitched four teams of mules. Two of the wagons, loaded with lighter goods, had teams of horses. The near wheel horse of each team was saddled for the teamster who would drive his team by the jerk line running to the bits of the lead teams. On each wagon a long leather brake strap extended from the brake pole and buckled on the saddle horn so that the teamster in the saddle could still brake his load.

A dozen teamsters and stevedores were gathered around the circular water tank in the wagon yard, watching Dave Harmon conduct a fairly routine chore.

Two of the teamsters, who had been drinking through the night, were ducking their heads in the trough and rubbing the backs of their necks in an attempt to sober up. The third man lay at their feet, dead drunk.

When the two teamsters came up sputtering, Dave regarded them critically.

"Well, if you can stand up, I reckon you can sit in a saddle. Now pitch him in," Dave said, indicating the teamster on the ground.

"No use, Dave. We had to carry him here," one teamster said.

"Throw him in anyway. At least it'll keep him cool for a few hours."

The two teamsters leaned unsteadily over their companion, seized him by arms and feet, lifted him up and rolled him over, face down, into the two feet of water in the big tank.

When the teamster did not struggle, Dave moved over swiftly, grasped the man's hair and lifted his head above water. The ducking, he saw, had not even succeeded in opening the man's eyes, and if he were left here he would drown.

"All right, pull him out, Solly," Dave ordered.

The two teamsters lifted out the dripping form of their companion and set him in the mud, his back propped against the tank. Dave looked about him at the circle of men. "I reckon you'll have to go in his place, Bailey." He had singled out a slight young man in rough clothes, who only nodded indifferently.

Now the teamster of the seventh wagon came into the yard and went directly up to Dave. "The escort just come, Dave. They're ready."

Dave looked at his men. "All right, let's go."

He went out through the gate and saw the escort waiting in the street. There were seven mounted troopers, and their sun-faded blue blouses were salty with dried perspiration from their ride down from Fort Mohave. They were armed with sabers, carbines, and pistols, and one of them was a bored and seasoned-looking, red-haired sergeant. Young Overman was leaning down, talking to John Thornton, who would drive the army ambulance in which he was seated. Beside him was Juliana Frost.

Dave touched his hat to Juliana.

Lieutenant Overman glanced beyond Dave and saw the teamsters mounting up as Dave said, "We're ready if you are, Lieutenant."

At that moment Thornton said to him, "Where do you want us, Lieutenant?"

Overman turned his head to look at Thornton. "Why, in the lead, so you're out of the dust. Move ahead slowly, Mister Thornton. We'll catch up with you." He turned to look at Dave. "You're sure we'll reach water tonight, Harmon?"

"I'm sure."

"I wish I weren't a stranger to this road," Overman said with wry good humor. "Looks like you'll be taking care of us instead of us taking care of you."

Dave smiled. "Not if it comes to trouble, Lieutenant," he said.

"Well, that's fair enough," Overman said. "You can take off now."

Harmon left him, and Overman pulled his horse around and rode back to his men. He named Sergeant Noonan and Trooper Cleary as advance guard, and called off the names of two more troopers who would serve as flankers. Then his orders put the detail in motion.

Just past the last house of Ehrenburg he caught up with the ambulance. Noonan and Cleary were riding a hundred yards ahead. Lieutenant Overman signaled out his flankers, then drew alongside the ambulance.

This wasn't much of an escort, First Lieutenant Richard Overman thought, and he wished that his first assignment since he received his promotion last month had been a less burdensome one. The reason for its being burdensome was seated beside John Thornton, he admitted to himself. He not only had the responsibility of protecting the teamsters, his own troopers, and a male passenger, but he had the added responsibility of protecting Juliana Frost, a major's daughter. In case of trouble what was the best way to protect her? She was a beautiful girl and, being army, she must certainly know that death was preferable to capture and torture by the Apaches. It wasn't that he was afraid she would be captured, though, but that she might be hurt in an exchange of gunfire.

He decided, then, that in case they were attacked the thing to do was to order Juliana to protect herself inside one of the freight wagons. He would ask Harmon if some freight couldn't be shifted to provide for this emergency. That, then, was settled.

This quick decision was characteristic of Lieutenant Overman. He was five years out of West Point and had served all of them in Western posts—in Dakota Territory, in Texas, and at Fort Mohave. The son of a wealthy New Yorker, he considered himself the most

unfortunate of men. His love affair with the Army had
begun at the age of three, lasted through the Civil War,
and would last as long as he lived, he knew. He had
spurned Harvard for West Point, over the objections
of his family. He had rejected all offers of his family to
use influence to get him soft, safe jobs in Eastern posts
or in Washington. Coming from the very lap of luxury,
he made a point of living on his lieutenant's pay. He
was, in short, doing exactly what he wanted to do,
with nobody's help and with nobody's advice.

One bit of luck that had come his way was his
promotion. It followed on the heels of the Army's
housecleaning of last year, when incompetent officers
were weeded out to make way for men of promise who
would build a better Army. All in all, Lieutenant Overman was a happy man—serious when he was practic-
ing the profession of arms, and lighthearted when he
was not.

Juliana Frost, despite the fact that this was not
the first trip she had made under military escort,
couldn't help but feel a quiet excitement this morning.
This was the last leg of a journey that began in New
York, traversed the Isthmus of Panama, to be resumed
on another voyage on the open seas, and in its next-
to-last stage saw her disembarkation from a schooner
onto a river steamboat. It seemed to her that she had
come halfway around the world so she could be again
with her parents.

It had been five years since she had seen them,
years that saw her graduate from a girl's school in New
York and then teach there. They had been good years
but lonely, and she had unaccountably missed the Army
life which, because of her years in an Eastern school,
she could only dimly remember. Now, just to listen to
Army talk, to discuss men she had known once and
forgotten, to share again in that friendly camaraderie
peculiar to service families, was a pleasant thing. The
past few days here, while miserably hot, had been en-
joyable. Part of the enjoyment, she suspected, was because young Overman, starved for the companionship

of women, had made her stay a gay one—he and John Thornton.

She glanced obliquely at Thornton, who was in easy conversation with Lieutenant Overman riding beside the ambulance. She and Thornton had met in Panama while both were waiting passage on the *Sprite*. When they discovered they were both headed for Fort Whipple, pleasant friendship began and was still maturing. He was a city man and make no pretense of being otherwise, yet he was tolerant of the rough frontier ways and was amused by them.

The lieutenant now dropped back to order flankers farther out as they entered broken and barren country.

"Where are they going?" Thornton asked.

"To watch for Indians," Juliana said.

"What if they find some?"

Juliana laughed. "They'll warn us in time so we're prepared for them. Indians like to surprise you. They don't like a set fight."

"And where did you learn all of this, Juliana?" Thornton asked, amusement in his voice.

"A thousand hours of listening."

Now Thornton's attention was diverted by the slowing of the ambulance. Neither Juliana nor Thornton had noticed they were entering a stretch of blow sand that made their sweating teams labor. The point troopers had crossed the long stretch of sand and reined up at its edge on the road ahead. When the ambulance crossed the blow sand, which sent up a stifling heat, wave after wave, Noonan raised a friendly hand to check them, and Thornton reined in.

"Sir, I think you and the lady had better wait here for a while. The wagons will have to double-team this blow sand and I don't think the lieutenant would like you to drive on alone."

"Thank you, Sergeant. We'll wait," Thornton said.

Noonan's prediction proved right. The heavy loads on the wagons mired them almost hub-deep in the sand, and Dave, taking spans from the other wagons, hitched them to each wagon to pull the load through the sand. Juliana, turning in her seat, watched the first wagon through. Dave was standing on his saddle so as to reach as far as he could toward the lead team with his long whip. As the wagon cleared the sand and the laboring horses came to a halt, Dave stepped down to unhook the lead teams. When he passed them Juliana noted that his shirt was plastered to his back with perspiration. He was so engrossed in his job that he paid them no attention.

"There's something strange about that man, John," she said. "You know he was a captain of cavalry before he left the service."

"I don't think I'd trade an officer's job for what he's doing now."

"According to Lieutenant Overman, I don't think he had any choice. With the sight of only one eye, the Army had to let him go."

Sergeant Noonan had dismounted now and was helping Dave unhitch the teams.

"What happened to blind him?" Thornton asked.

"Fighting the Sioux," Dick Overman said.

"Well, what's strange about him, except he's half blind?" Thornton asked drily.

Juliana thought a moment. "Doesn't it seem strange to you that a man with West Point training should settle for this?"

Thornton smiled. "Come to think of it, it does seem strange. You'd think his education would qualify him to be an engineer or a lawyer. He should be in a profession."

"I feel sorry for him," Juliana said.

"I wouldn't let him know you do," Thornton said. "He strikes me as a man who isn't looking for pity."

Now Dave, driving the extra teams back, passed them again, and again he did not look at them. Oddly, his concentration on the task at hand made Juliana feel useless and almost frivolous.

Troopers Reardon and Adams had left the detail at the water hole after sundown. Their orders were simple. They were to travel north at night by moonlight, using Lieutenant Miller's hand compass as a guide, and walk until they intercepted the stage road. When eventually they reached help, they were to report their compass reading so that the rescuers could locate the detail. Reardon could not read a compass nor be taught how to read one, so the task fell on young Trooper Adams.

As darkness fell and moonlight replaced daylight, it seemed to Trooper Adams that he and Reardon were the only two men alive, and that they were traversing the face of the moon.

After what they judged to be an hour, but was only half an hour, they rested. Reardon's friends had polled together their tobacco so that his pocket bulged with plugs. Now he cut off a corner, lifted it to his mouth, tucked it in his jaw, then carefully licked the knife before putting it away.

A lean man with a dark, ravaged face, Reardon had served in the Army seventeen of the forty years of his life, having re-enlisted three times under different names. Although he hated army life and suffered its hardships grudgingly, he knew that he was doomed to remain in it until he died. There was a reason for his certain knowledge; he could not live outside the Army.

Three times he had tried to leave it and each time he had failed, for Trooper Reardon had a love for drink that could not be appeased. Each time he had been separated from the Army with a little money, and each time he spent the money on a spree. Sick, sodden with whiskey, he was unable to find anything but the most menial work. Whatever he earned at these jobs went not for food and clothing, but for more whiskey. Eventually, barely able to drag himself to the nearest place of recruitment, he enlisted again.

Reardon had found that with few interruptions, such as this detail, he could stay quietly drunk on an army post. There was always the sutler's store or the cheap saloons called "hog pens" off the post where whiskey could be bought. The Army clothed him and fed him and did not work him hard enough to bother him. The trick was to drink just enough so as not to attract notice. A few times when he drank too much, he cheerfully served extra duty or time in the guardhouse, where his friends smuggled in whiskey. The Army, mercifully, was fairly tolerant of drinking by enlisted men, and it had its own control of sorts. This control consisted of paying its men so little that it was hard to afford the luxury of drink.

Now Trooper Reardon placidly softened his chew of tobacco with the few teeth left him. He really had not minded drawing the next to shortest straw this morning. It meant that if he lived, he would be again close to whiskey far sooner than his companions. If he died, then his companions would die too. Besides, he had a secret.

Reardon spat. "The lieutenant kept telling us to watch the country, watch the shape of it, so we'd recognize it on the trip back. You see any shape to this country, sonny?"

"My name is Jack," Trooper Adams said quietly.

"All right, sonny, it's Jack."

"No, I don't see no shape to it," Trooper Adams said.

No seventeen-year-old has much of a history, and Trooper Adams had less than most. He was slight, barely the Army's minimum height, and no amount of exposure to the desert sun could tan his narrow, sallow face. Left an orphan at three, he had no family of any sort. To this day he did not know who had placed him in the Ohio orphanage where he spent his first fourteen years. It had been a heartless place, and Trooper Adams' small stature was probably due to the wretched and inadequate food of that institution.

As far back as he could remember he had feared and disliked adults, and a good bit of his life had been dedicated to evading their orders, lying to them, stealing from them, and confusing them.

When, at the age of fifteen, the orphanage dismissed him as of working age, there was no place for him to go. He knew no trade or occupation save that of a kitchen helper and truck gardener. His meager schooling had been careless and had been received half-heartedly by him. Joining the Army then was a natural solution, he reasoned. There he would be fed, housed, and paid. His genuine talent for avoiding work and his sharp instinct for survival would get him by.

It had turned out just that way. His total lack of

responsibility, his cunning doging of work, his distrust of his superiors and even of his equals guaranteed that he would be disliked and never promoted. In two years the thought of desertion had never occurred to him, for in the world outside the Army, work was demanded of all if they were to eat.

He had not been surprised when he had drawn the short stick. All his life he had been receiving some form of the short stick, so why shouldn't it happen this time? It really didn't matter to him, for he had a simple conviction, stemming from his youth and experience, that he would survive. This belief, coupled with his native shrewdness, his selfishness, and his tough young body actually made him an excellent, if unplanned, choice for this mission.

Now Trooper Adams twisted one of the canteens around his belly, unscrewed the cap and took a drink of water. Reardon, observing him, reached back for one of his canteens, unscrewed the cap and took a healthy swig.

Trooper Adams lifted his head and began to sniff. "What's the funny smell?" he said.

"Whiskey," Reardon said calmly.

Adams slowly capped his canteen by feel; he was watching Reardon almost with disbelief.

"Where'd you get any whiskey?" he demanded.

"Now, you've been with me for a week, sonny. Where do you think I got it?"

"Brought it with you?"

"Course I brought it with me. You never see an officer sniff a man's canteen, do you?"

"But what've you done for water?"

"Another canteen, sonny. Haven't you noticed a lot of the boys carry an extra?"

Trooper Adams had no reply to this, but a feeling of uneasiness came to him. He had a premonition that this journey would require stamina and would push them to the limits of their endurance. He also knew that alcohol and the blasting desert daytime heat did not mix. He felt he should caution Reardon, but he did not want to antagonize the older trooper so early in their association.

"You been drinking that stuff every day?" Adams asked.

Reardon chuckled. "Oh, I'd take a nip when I was alone or on sentry duty. No use saving it now though." He looked at Adams. "I don't figure you're the kind to report me."

"No," Adams agreed.

"Wouldn't do you any good anyway. By the time we reach help, it'll be gone."

"You ought to go easy on it, though," Adams said.

"I was living with this stuff before you were born, sonny. Just don't try and teach your grandmother how to suck eggs."

"Sure," Trooper Adams said meekly. Now he rose. "Well, the sooner we start off, the sooner we'll get there."

"No denying it," Reardon agreed. He got up, hitched up his belt, and together they marched off into the north.

At noon next day, after a morning of blazing heat in which they had seen no living thing except an occasional high, curious vulture, the road dipped down into the barren Possos Valley to the well at Tyson. Here was blessed shade among the stunted cottonwoods and an opportunity for the train to water their teams and mounts. The troopers naturally clustered with the teamsters and away from their officer. Lieutenant Overman was helping John Thornton lay out a blanket for a picnic spread. The troopers began stolidly to eat their bacon and bread.

Dave climbed up on a wheel of his wagon, reached in his grub box, and brought out the beef sandwiches with which he had stocked up in Ehrenburg. They were edible for only a day or so in this smothering heat, but they saved making a fire in a land that was hot enough already, and one in which a man had to carry his own fuel. Cooking would come later when he had run out of prepared provisions. He was headed for the group of teamsters and troopers when Lieutenant Overman called out, "Oh, Harmon, come join us, won't you?"

Dave halted, and hesitated almost too long. He did

not really want to join them, and during his hesitation he wondered why this was. He supposed it was because there was a better than even chance he would be quizzed about his Army past, which he did not especially want to discuss. On the other hand, he did not wish to appear unnecessarily rude, so he veered to his right, saying, "Glad to."

When he approached and Juliana saw the sandwiches in his parcel, she said, "There's more than enough here. Why don't you save your food, Captain?"

Here it comes, Dave thought. He removed his hat, sat down, and said pleasantly, "Not captain any more, Miss Frost. I might as well eat my food before it spoils."

"All ex-Army men are called by their rank, I always thought," Juliana said.

"I'd reckon that was a hangover from the war," Dave said. "Nowadays there aren't any misters except old men. All the rest are majors, captains, lieutenants, or sergeants." He paused. "It's a custom that takes the honor away from the rank, I think."

He began to eat while Juliana studied him with a faint curiosity. "I'd never thought of that," she said slowly. "It does seem unfair to the field soldier to address him by the same title you use to a pot-bellied banker who got a Civil War commission by raising his own company."

"But what if the banker served his country honorably?" John Thornton put in. "Isn't he entitled to be called by his rank?"

"But now he's a civilian," Dave said. "He isn't serving his country any more, but there are men who are. They are the ones entitled to be addressed by rank."

"I'll go farther than that," Lieutenant Overman said, and his pale eyes held a glint of humor. "Rank is for the military structure only. It's only sensible use is to Army personnel, because it tells who's in charge over whom. Outside of that, I can't see any use for it, not even for cotillions. The higher your rank, the uglier girls you draw. It's the second lieutenents who always have the prettiest girls."

Juliana laughed. "Just how would you like to be addressed, Lieutenant Overman?"

"As Dick. It was good enough for my mother, and it should be good enough for all of you."

They all laughed quietly, except Thornton. Juliana turned to Dave. "Are you of Dick's school, Mister Harmon?" At Dave's nod of assent, she said, "Then it's Dick, Dave, and John. That should make me Juliana to all of you."

"*Miss* Juliana," Overman corrected her. "Women have to be addressed by rank so we men know who we're free to kiss or to propose to."

Juliana chuckled, but there was a frown on Thornton's face. Lieutenant Overman's harmless whimsy and gallantry apparently did not amuse him, Dave noted.

At that moment Sergeant Noonan approached the group, came to attention, and saluted. "Permission to relieve Carruthers, sir."

Lieutenant Overman looked up, slightly startled. "Why, Sergeant?"

"I've eaten, sir. He's still out on the flank."

"Permission granted," Lieutenant Overman said. "Get somebody to relieve Malone, too. Leave your sabers and bring in theirs. They're only a nuisance in this heat."

As Noonan went over to his horse, Overman said, "He looks like a good man. I wish he were in our troop."

"Isn't he?" Juliana asked.

"No, he's at Whipple. Been on leave and is only traveling with us."

Dave looked off and studied Noonan as he mounted and rode out toward the bluff. "That's a good horse, and not Army branded."

Lieutenant Overman nodded. "He explained that. It's his own. Since he's on leave and not on duty, I reckon that's his own affair."

Dave only nodded, but as he watched Noonan ride out to relieve Carruthers, he wondered. A cavalry trooper's pay, even a sergeant's, was too meager to afford a horse as good as this one. Still, Dave remembered, a good gambler trooper who stayed sober could parlay a small stake into a sizable sum. When a trooper did, he usually deserted because he had the money to get him away from a locality where he could be apprehended. On the other hand, some good gamblers stuck with the Army for the simple reason that while paymasters on their rounds seldom visit army posts, when they did they left a substantial sum with the troopers. If a good gambler got to the troopers before they had drunk up their back pay, he could come off a big winner. Since this sergeant was returning to his post and riding an excellent horse, the chances were he was one of the better and shrewder gamblers.

They ate in silence for a moment, and then Thornton said abruptly, "Tell me, Captain, how did you get in the freighting business?"

Dave's single eye regarded him coldly. "Why, the way you get in any business. I bought into it."

"But why in Ehrenburg?" Thornton persisted.

"Lord, yes, why there?" Lieutenant Overman added.

Dave knew what they meant and smiled faintly, his resentment at Thornton's impertinent question dissolving.

"The freight for the north part of the whole territory comes through Ehrenburg. I've hauled as far as New Mexico," Dave said, adding, "Somebody's got to haul it. It might as well be my outfit."

"I'd never have guessed that," Juliana said.

"Neither did I until I was stationed in New Mexico. When you wait on guns and ammunition you're pretty sure to know where they come from. They come from Ehrenburg."

"Any to Edwards at Whipple in this load?" Thornton asked.

Dave shook his head.

"What do you charge for the freight you're hauling?" Thornton asked.

"Five cents a pound."

"And that's cheaper than the Army can haul its own goods?"

"They must think so, or they wouldn't have contracted me," Dave said.

"Doesn't Edwards have his own freight wagons?" Thornton persisted.

Dave said, "He tried it, but it was too expensive. He wasn't big enough to keep teams, wagons, and teamsters busy freighting the year round. As a matter of fact, I bought four wagons from him when I started freighting."

"Five cents a pound seems outrageous," Thornton said bluntly. "I'm going to look into his figures."

"You don't have to," Dave said. "When he freighted his own goods, they cost him sixteen cents a pound laid down at Whipple."

"It wouldn't cost me that," Thornton said. "I'm too good a businessman to tolerate that."

"So was Edwards," Dave said drily. "That's why he's contracting his freighting."

By now Dave was of the opinion that he had antagonized Thornton in some way he didn't understand. He wondered if Thornton had held a Civil War commission and secretly wished to be addressed by his rank. Perhaps Dave's words had goaded him into the unpleasantness. It didn't matter, Dave thought, since he'd see as little of Thornton as possible on this trip.

When the train formed for the afternoon, Noonan was kept as the right flanker. His thoughts turned now to the presence of the girl in the train. This presented a problem, but only one of sorts. If his men had to lay siege to the train the girl would inevitably be in danger, and he wondered if his men would remember her presence. He was sure they would, for he had left instructions with Kirby to have a man watching his departure, so Kirby would know the number he was up against.

Kirby, too, had turned out to be a problem, but one that was easily disposed of. Once the rifles were in hand it would be easy enough to provoke Kirby into a gun fight, or even ambush him.

All in all, Noonan thought, this job should be fairly easy. The detail was small, and the teamsters wouldn't contribute much. Doubtless Harmon was capable, but his men wouldn't die for him. Harmon, he judged, would be the man to watch and, if possible, to kill first. He knew nothing of Harmon except from hearsay, but already Harmon was indirectly responsible for the death of two of his men. Noonan wished now he had checked more thoroughly on this taciturn one-eyed man. He had thought he would be dealing with average riffraff teamsters who were not about to lay down their lives for a wagonload of groceries, or even rifles. Now he was dealing with the freight-line owner, who had not only his freight but his reputation at stake. He would have to learn more about the man from the troopers when they camped tonight.

All through the afternoon Noonan kept a sharp lookout. Once he saw some dust in the broken country to the south, but it was a dust devil.

They made camp that night on a rocky bench below which was a bitter spring whose water the animals disliked but drank. Afterwards a rope corral was fashioned, the anchor posts being the wagons, and the horses and mules were turned into it. Two separate fires were built, one for the soldiers and the teamsters, the other for the lieutenant, Juliana, and Thornton. Harmon, Noonan was happy to see, was going to eat with his teamsters. As daylight faded, Lieutenant Overman put out two sentries to guard the corral.

One of the troopers volunteered as cook, and the teamsters' rations were thrown in with the Army's. Harmon was seated cross-legged on the ground talking to one of his men. Watching him, Noonan wondered curiously if the loss of the sight of one eye wasn't a considerable handicap. *Well, there was one way to find out,* Noonan thought.

Very quietly, he moved over to Harmon's left. There were half a dozen conversations going on and Noonan was certain that his approach was undetected, yet he was a bare six feet away when Harmon turned and looked at him.

Noonan said affably, "I just wondered how far you reckon we made it today."

"I'd judge twelve to fifteen miles, Sergeant."

"That's about what I figured."

"We won't make that tomorrow," the other said. "We've got more sand coming up."

Noonan shook his head. "Don't see how you fellows buck this country," he said pleasantly. "At Whipple we've at least got some shade."

"Captain Carter still at Whipple, Sergeant?"

Noonan thought quickly. "I don't think he'll be there when I get back from leave. There was talk of a transfer when I left."

Harmon nodded indifferently. Was Harmon trying to trap him, Noonan wondered. Did he suspect there was something strange about him?

Noonan moved away. No, he was imagining things, but still he'd better keep away from Harmon. After tonight, though, Noonan knew Harmon would no longer be concerned with his white little lies.

When supper was finished the two teamsters who had started out drunk this morning rolled up in their blankets under one of the wagons and went to sleep, Dave observed. Now he watched Thornton and the lieutenant stringing up a blanket from the front to the rear wheel of the supply wagon. Later a folding cot was hauled out from the ambulance and placed behind the blanket. He supposed this would be Juliana's bedroom this night.

Singly and in pairs the teamsters and troopers began to desert the fires for their blankets. Dave moved over to his wagon and was lifting down his blanket roll when he saw Juliana moving toward the wagon. When he stepped down, she had halted. The fire behind her made a corona of her pale hair.

"You deserted us for supper, Dave."

Dave said patiently, "No, I didn't desert you. I'm a teamster, Miss Juliana."

"What's that supposed to mean?" Juliana asked.

"Only that you're a guest of the Army, and I work for them."

"But you *were* an officer," Juliana persisted.

"So were a lot of men. I daresay some of them are in jail now."

She had no reply for that, but Dave could see a faint resentment in her face. He noted that Thornton was watching them, a scowl on his soft face. Perhaps he had been overly blunt with this girl, Dave thought, but he did not want to be put in a false position. While she was pleasant and very likely good company, he could tell that Thornton had assumed a proprietary interest in her. Dave's presence at their shared meals would make for an increasing awkwardness as the days went on. It was much simpler to settle it now.

"Are there Apaches this close to Ehrenburg?" Juliana asked quietly.

"They're where you find them," Dave said. "The only good thing about them is that they won't fight at night."

"At least we sleep, then," Juliana said.

Dave nodded. "They like the first light."

Juliana shivered a little, but Dave felt it was from the night chill, not fear.

"Then beware the first light, is that it?"

"That's for the Army to worry about, not you," Dave said, and smiled faintly.

Juliana smiled then, too, and said good night. She turned and walked back to the fire to join Thornton. Lieutenant Overman was out checking on his sentries. When Juliana came up to the fire she noted the frown on Thornton's face. He was seated on a saddle and got up when she came over.

"You think that's wise, Juliana?" he asked quietly.

Juliana gave him a blank look.

"Talking with Harmon, I mean," Thornton continued. "That may give some of these men a wrong impression."

"Of me?" There was incredulity in Juliana's voice.

"It just doesn't look right," Thornton insisted. "He runs a rough lot of men in a rough business. If they see him taking liberties they will, too."

Anger came into Juliana's eyes. "Just how is he taking liberties, John?"

"Talking to you."

"But I went up and talked with him."

"That makes no difference. If he feels free to associate with you, they will, too."

"But he was a captain in the Army!" Juliana protested.

Thornton's voice was almost cool. "Right now he's

one of seven rough, dirty teamsters. I just don't think you should associate with him, Juliana."

"Apparently he thinks the same thing, John. So, all right, I won't associate with him and he won't associate with me. Now, I'm going to bed. Good night."

"Good night, Juliana." Thornton watched her as she walked over to the supply wagon, and on his face was an expression of lingering petulance.

3

By the time Dave laid out his blanket roll and eased out of his boots, both fires were dying down and a waning moon had risen. He suddenly remembered that it was time for the test which he set himself each month. He shoved his eyepatch up onto his forehead, then closed his good eye. With his injured eye he could see a light patch which was the moon, but which was dim and a little blurred. *Better than last month,* he thought, and he slipped the patch down into place and rolled into his blankets.

Why, he wondered, did Doc Hartley, contract surgeon at Fort Yuma, insist that the injured eye be covered? Muscles only strengthened with use, so why not eyes? Dr. Hartley's explanation was that the savage sun glare under which Dave regularly worked would only inflame the injured eye, and this inflammation might eventually lead to total blindness. Maybe he was right, Dave thought, but he wondered on what distant day he could discard this cumbersome eyepatch. To him it was a symbol of bad luck and a reminder of what might have been, rather than a mark of inadequacy. It was easier to forget the past if there was nothing in the present to remind you of it. The eyepatch was his constant reminder.

But it really didn't matter, he thought. If he'd remained in the Army, he might have a command by now. It might well be a field command, or it might equally well be a dreary tour of duty at a remount station. No matter what a man did, it all came out the same—hanging on in bad times, crowding luck when it came your way. He supposed, when he stopped to think of it, that these were good times for him. He was driving himself and his men and making money. Where it would be spent he hadn't stopped to consider.

Memory of Juliana Frost's words crossed his mind then. *But you were a captain.* That implied that he was a gentleman fit to associate not only with her but with her beloved army people and with John Thornton. If he had not once been a captain of cavalry, would she have bothered being pleasant to him? In all honesty, he had to tell himself he thought she would. Army women, while clannish, were usually a proud yet humble lot. They met a greater variety of men than their sisters, and if there was character in them they profited by this fact. To be even connected with the Army was to have an understanding and tolerance of man's foibles and weaknesses.

Dave turned over and slept.

He did not know how much later it was that a shot, and a close one, wakened him. He came out of his blankets and at the same time he heard the milling and the whinnying of frightened horses and mules. Swiftly jamming his feet into his boots, he grabbed his hat and gun belt and ran for the corral, strapping on his gun as he ran. Now the sound of milling became the sound of running. Other more distant shots ripped the night, and Dave heard Overman's wild voice yelling, "Over here, men!"

Dave raced for the corral, the faint moonlight allowing him to see ahead. A bullet resounded boomingly off one of the high-sided freight wagons.

When he rounded one of the anchor wagons for the corral he saw the horses and mules boiling out of it at a dead run. He ran toward the galloping herd which was streaming through a break in the rope corral. They seemed to be avoiding something that lay on the ground, and as a horse swerved toward him Dave ran alongside him, grabbed his mane, let his weight go slack, and thrust his feet ahead of him. Then, lowering his feet, he dug his heels into the dirt. The onrushing of the horse threw Dave's legs high in the air so that he was lifted astraddle the horse.

He needed no reins now, for the horses and mules were bunched in running panic, his own mount at the very edge of it. Behind him, distant now, he heard more shooting. From his opposite side Dave picked up the sound of running animals and he leaned low over his mount's neck, searching the darkness on his right. Suddenly, out of it loomed two riders at a dead gallop, their forms partially obscured by the dust raised by the horses ahead. These were not his men nor soldiers of the detail, and they seemed determined to catch up with the leaders.

As they came even with him and were about to pass him, Dave drew his gun. He snapped a shot at the nearest rider and saw the nearest horse go down in front of the second horse. The rider simply pinwheeled over the horse's head before it hit the ground. The second horse piled into the first, stumbled, and went down. An orange light blossomed in the night from the second rider. And now Dave emptied his gun. He saw the stumbling horse rise and the rider mount, then they swerved off in the direction from which they had come, to be swallowed in darkness.

The stampeding animals, turning away from the sound of the shooting, were now headed east. They were tiring, Dave saw, and their pace was slacking off. Slowly he worked his way up to the lead horses that had fallen into a steady lope. He kneed his own horse into the nearest leader and they gave way gradually until Dave was forcing them into a wide circle. The mules and horses behind were following the leaders, their panic slowly dying down. In another twenty minutes the leaders were traveling at a walk.

Now Dave put his mind to what had happened. It was unlikely their attackers were Indians. An Apache would steal horses at night, but he would not fight, believing that death in darkness was death eternal. Memory went back to the attempted robbery of the warehouse. Was there a connection? Morning, he thought, would tell, for he was sure that the rider of the horse he had downed was either afoot or hurt.

He listened for further shooting, but the racket made on the rocky ground by the herd of horses smothered any other sound.

When the lead horses refused to turn further, Dave put his own horse out ahead and the herd followed docilely. There was no forage and no water to distract them.

It was perhaps a half-hour later when Dave saw the trio of men afoot loom out of the faint moonlight ahead of him.

"Sing out!" someone called.

If this was the enemy, Dave figured he could lose himself quickly in the herd behind him. If they were friends they were blessedly welcome. Caution, however, prompted Dave's answer. "You sing out. I'm alone."

"This is Lieutenant Overman," the voice called.

Dave answered with his own name, and he rode up to two troopers flanking Lieutenant Overman.

"Thank God you got the horses," Overman said fervently. "I figured we were afoot. We hoped we could pick up a few strays."

"Is anybody hurt?" Dave asked.

"Molvaney, one of the sentries, was stomped into the rock. One of your men got a leg wound. Outside of that we're all right." Overman paused. "Harmon, we counted twelve rifles. What do you figure? Apaches?"

"I don't think so. The men I saw weren't, but come daylight we can find out. If I were you I'd send a couple of men to follow the tracks the herd made last night. Somewhere along the trail they'll find a downed horse. Maybe a hurt man, too. That should tell us what we want to know."

"Good," Overman said. Then he spoke to the troopers. "Cut three horses out of that bunch and let's get moving." When the two troopers moved in among the animals, they had little difficulty in finding docile mounts. They were carrying bridles, and the first horse bridled was turned over to the lieutenant. Then, with a trooper on either side, Overman in the lead, Dave in the drag, they drove the herd in the direction of the camp.

Behind them, to the east, was the first gray of false dawn.

It was dawn when they hit the wagon road, and full daylight when they rode into camp. Fresh fires were built and Dave saw that the remaining troopers, plus a couple of his conscripted freighters, were staked out in a wide circle around the camp, waiting for the developments of the day.

Dave slipped off the durable pony he had used and it joined the herd. Looking about him, he saw that Juliana and Thornton, with the aid of a trooper, had taken over the breakfast chore for the whole camp. One by one the guards were whistled in to eat. While the remuda was being watered, the first two men finished with breakfast were ordered by Overman to ride out on the tracks of the stampeding herd and search for the downed horse and rider. As the teamsters and troopers finished their breakfast they grained their horses in preparation for the day's drive.

Meanwhile Dave had gone over to the supply wagon where he was told the wounded teamster was lying. It turned out to be Everts, one of the men who had shown up drunk yesterday. He had a nasty gouge in his thigh from an almost spent bullet, but his bearded face held more worry than pain. His wound had been bandaged, and when Dave asked how he felt he spat elaborately over the side of the wagon before he answered.

"I'm all right, Dave. I can drive." He paused. "Them wasn't Injuns."

"We'll know for sure in a little while," Dave answered. "What have you got on that leg?"

"That-there lady put flour on the cut. It sure stopped the bleeding."

Only then did Dave move over to the fire. The troopers and teamsters trekking in for food accepted their food and moved off by themselves. Now Lieutenant Overman took two plates, offered Dave one, had his plate filled by Juliana, and then firmly took her by the arm and led her to a blanket spread on the ground. Dave helped himself and was preparing to move over with the troopers when his glance lifted to Juliana. She looked pale and somehow forlorn in this early sun. Smudges of ashes were on her face and her arms. Impulsively he went over and sat down beside her.

"That first light came awful early, Dave," she said drily.

"Didn't it?" Dave agreed. He knew she was referring to what he had said last night about the timing of Apache attacks. But, waiting proof, he refused to let himself be baited.

"This can happen every night, can't it?" Juliana asked.

"I don't think Overman will let it happen."

"How will he stop it?"

"Form a corral of all wagons with the horses inside, I reckon," Dave said. He glanced curiously at her. "Where were you last night?"

"They made me lie in the supply wagon," Juliana said slowly. She looked up at him. "I can shoot."

"That's for soldiers," Dave said gruffly.

John Thornton moved over and wearily sat down beside Juliana. He looked more tired than she, as if the events of last night had impressed upon him that this was more than an uncomfortable ride in a borrowed ambulance.

"Harmon, I guess we're all in your debt for saving those horses and teams."

"I had a little stake in keeping them myself," Dave said drily.

"I heard that the Apaches go for the horses first."

"They do," Dave said noncommittally. He drank the last of his coffee and got up.

Dave first hooked up Everts' teams and then his own. He didn't intend that Everts should drive even if the teamster wanted to, and now he was faced with finding another teamster. As he worked, he noted that a quartet of troopers were piling rocks on the trampled remains of Molvaney in a makeshift grave. Nobody knew if Molvaney had mercifully been killed by the first shot, but the whole camp hoped so, in view of what had happened to him later.

Already the sun was blasting hot, and everyone, teamsters and soldiers alike, was anxious to break camp.

It was while the wagons were waiting to form up that the two troopers sent on reconnaissance pulled into sight. Dave went over to where Lieutenant Overman, Juliana, and Thornton were standing.

The two riders, one of them Sergeant Noonan, rode directly to Lieutenant Overman to report. Sergeant Noonan properly saluted. "We found the downed man, sir. Apparently he broke his neck from the fall."

"A white man?" Overman asked quickly.

Noonan nodded and extended a battered hat containing a few personal belongings—a knife, a plug of tobacco, some small coins, and a polished buckeye, a good-luck piece that had probably been swapped with some immigrant.

"His horse was dead, too," Noonan continued. "The gear wasn't worth salvaging."

"All right, Sergeant," Overman said. Noonan and the trooper withdrew, and Lieutenant Overman stared glumly at the hat and the assorted contents; then his glance lifted to Dave. "What do you figure, Dave?"

"I think somebody wants our train." Dave's voice was matter-of-fact.

"Nonsense," Thornton said sharply. "Why would a dozen men kill people for nails and sugar and rope?"

"We've got other freight, Thornton," Dave said, and he paused to emphasize his next word. "One hundred and fifty rifles. Remember, my warehouse was raided in Yuma. Surely you heard about that."

At Thornton's nod, Dave continued, "I didn't know what they were after, and neither did Lieutenant Overman. You figured they were after the usual loot—whiskey or whatever they could sell."

Juliana had been listening intently, and now she said, "Now we know."

"I think we do," Overman said glumly.

"Why, who'd buy rifles?" Thornton asked.

"Apaches use them, I'm told."

Watching this information sink into Thornton's mind, Dave waited for his reaction to it once it was digested.

Overman said bitterly, "We should have been allowed a bigger escort."

Dave made no comment, although he agreed.

Lieutenant Overman looked about him, grim decision in his thin face. "Well, we'll make do with what we have." He looked abruptly at Harmon. "You think they'll hang on?"

Dave shrugged. "I can't tell you, Dick. You'll have to wait and see. There's mighty little traveling on this road nowadays. Still, with all that freight moving out upriver there should be trains behind us, but they'll be waiting on an escort."

"You're suggesting we wait?" Thornton asked.

"I'm suggesting nothing," Dave said flatly.

A faint anger at the world in general stirred in Overman's face. "Damned if we will! No civilian is going to escort the Army." He turned to Juliana. "Can you handle that ambulance team, Miss Frost?"

"Of course. I drove part of the way yesterday."

"And you, Thornton," Overman continued, "can you drive the supply wagon?"

"I'm sure I can."

"That'll free one man to take the hurt teamster's place. Which reminds me, there'll be a short service for Molvaney before we pull out."

It was short, too. The troopers and all the men, save Everts, stood bareheaded around the high mound of rocks while Overman recited a short prayer. A crude cross of wood from a crate was tied together by leather thongs, and this, supported by rocks, stood at the head of the surface grave.

Afterward Overman sent out his flankers and the train pulled out into the blistering heat of the day. Dave, again in the lead wagon, wondered what he would do in Overman's place. It depended, he supposed, on what lay in the future. But the trouble with what lay in the future, he thought wryly, is that when it happened it was too late to act in the past.

Kirby gave the train plenty of time to assemble and move out before he rode in to Tyson Wells. He had sent his men into the rocky foothills of the nearby Granite Wash Mountains with orders to wait for him.

Last night's failure was rankling him and he was

in a surly temper. To have come so close to success and then to have fumbled the opportunity was a galling memory. If they had succeeded in leaving the train afoot, it would have been a simple enough matter to set siege to the train, and either reduce them or accept their surrender. Now that all had to be done over again, and Kirby was in a quandary. He and his men did not carry enough food for themselves and their horses to make a sustained and prolonged attack.

The reason for his return to the Wells was that he was certain Brick would communicate with him by some means. He hoped he was right, because he was frankly at a loss as to the next move.

He reined in now and regarded the camp site. He looked at the remains of the two fires and the horse-trampled ground. No camp of soldiers or teamsters was ever free of the litter of tin cans, empty bottles, and trash. This camp was no exception. Kirby rode his horse to the rocked-in well under the stunted cottonwoods, and while the horse was drinking, he went back to the camp site. It would have helped if he knew what he was looking for and if he was certain there would be a message. Could it be scribbled in the dust? He didn't think so, since writing it would have drawn attention to Brick.

He picked up a can and looked inside and saw it was empty and discarded it. He did the same with a pair of whiskey bottles. Then his roving glance settled on an upright can on the edge of the cold fire. He walked over to it and picked it up and saw that it was a can that had held tomatoes. Its label was jammed inside it. He had his hand raised to throw the can away when he halted the motion. He pulled out the label and turned it over. There, written on the back of the label, was the message he had been waiting for: *Circle and fight them off King Wells*. It was unsigned, of course.

Kirby tore up the note, then headed back for his horse, pondering the wisdom of Brick's instructions. Obviously, what Brick hoped they could do was to keep the train from water until heat and thirst beat it into submission. The question was, could his fourteen men—no, thirteen, for Hallam was killed last night—

hold off a slightly superior force? He supposed it all depended on the topography of the land where the next water was.

He was almost to the spring when he heard the distant hoofbeats of horses. The sound came from the east, but his sight was obscured by the young cottonwoods crowding the well.

His men? he wondered angrily. He had told them to wait for his gun-shot signal to approach and water their horses.

He moved away from the well into the open. In the distance he could see the approaching westbound stage and its escort of five troopers. For a moment Kirby hesitated. Should he get out of here on the run? He quickly decided against it. He had a right to travel the country, and since nobody had seen him last night they could not possibly have a description of him. He was filling the canteen above his horse at the head of the seep when the stage and its escort rolled in.

At sight of him, the sergeant in command of the troopers signaled a halt and the stage driver pulled up. A couple of curious men passengers looked out the curtained end windows as the sergeant rode over. He was as burly as Kirby, and some five years younger. His uniform was dusty, and as he approached he pulled down a yellow handkerchief from the lower part of his face.

Kirby rose, canteen in hand. "Morning, soldier."

"You alone?" the sergeant demanded.

Kirby turned and looked around him. "I thought I was. You see anybody else with me?"

"What are you doing here?"

Kirby said pointedly, "Minding my own damn business. Try it some time."

"Where you headed for?"

Kirby gave him a long, level look. "You sound as if you wanted to stop me wherever I'm going. I wouldn't advise you to try it."

Surprisingly, the sergeant smiled. "Hell, I'm not stopping you. The thing is, we just passed a wagon train heading for Whipple. They were attacked here last night."

"Injuns?"

"They didn't think so. A bunch of roughs after
the trade goods. You're liable to run into them if you
hang around here."

"Well, I don't aim to hang around here, soldier.
I'm headed east."

"Then you better hurry and catch up with that
train. A single rider is a sittin' duck for the 'Paches."

"You see any?" Kirby asked.

The sergeant nodded. "A small bunch followed us
for half a day, then veered off north. We had too many
guns, I reckon."

Kirby seemed to consider this. "Where's the next
water?"

"Layton's Place."

"That a stage station?"

The sergeant nodded. "Eight miles or so from
here."

"And after that, where?"

"A long haul to King's Wells. No station there."

Kirby asked irrelevantly, "The Apaches hittin' any
of the stage stations?"

"They tried Layton's last week. They pulled out
when they lost a couple of men." He added, "No, sir,
mister, I wouldn't travel alone. Catch up with that
train."

"Reckon I will," Kirby said.

The trooper gestured loosely, wheeled his horse,
and went back to the stage, which was already moving. It sounded to Kirby as if King's Wells would be
the place to keep a train from water, since there was
no station there and the train couldn't expect help. The
train would probably noon at the stage station at Layton's and push on for King's Wells. They would have
had a long drive and would be in real need of water.

Now Kirby pulled out a cigar, lighted it, and
lolled in the shade. When it was half smoked, he drew
his gun and fired twice. Even if the troopers heard the
shots, they would do nothing. Their orders undoubtedly
were to protect the stage and its passengers.

Before his cigar was finished, his men began to
trail in from their hiding place in the rocks. There

wasn't a dry thread on them, Kirby noted, and their horses were sweating too. He knew that the furnace heat of the rocks had tortured them, but he also knew that had Overman decided to snoop around for his attackers last night he would look in vain in the rocks. Simple robbery, Kirby concluded wryly, was not always simple in this country.

An hour after the train had broken camp the heat was blazing down without mercy. When Juliana looked to the right and left at the far-out flankers, they appeared as wavy uncertain objects. Although she would not admit it to herself, she was exhausted this morning. Every member of the train had spent an uneasy night after the attempted horse raid, she suspected.

Glancing behind her at the supply wagon driven by Thornton, she saw Lieutenant Overman in conversation with him. She was oddly relieved that she was free of John and alone today, for since her near quarrel with him last evening she felt a little less friendly toward him. She supposed that his objection to her talking with Dave Harmon stemmed only from his desire to protect her, nevertheless there was an implicit snobbery in his words. He did not understand what everyone else in the West knew without ever stating it: a respectable woman in this country was perfectly safe in the hands of the most desperate killers except Indians.

She corrected herself, thinking, *What about last night's raid?* Certainly the attackers were shooting indiscriminately at the camp, and their bullets could have hit her as easily as the teamster who was hit. It was a sobering thought. Also, if the raiders had succeeded in stealing their horses, they would have spent not only uncomfortable but dangerous hours in this desert before help could be brought. It was only because of Dave Harmon that they had not succeeded.

She wondered now about him and speculated on what series of events had turned him into the cross-grained, distant, almost unfriendly man that he appeared to be. Was he jealous of Lieutenant Overman's command? She doubted that. In his army career he had commanded far more men in far more dangerous situations. Was he envious or scornful of Lieutenant Overman's youth? She doubted that too, since he was young enough himself not to consider Lieutenant Overman extremely young. Shrewdly she guessed that perhaps his forced retirement from the Army might be at the core of his actions. When a man was doing superbly the one thing he wished to do, it could be a bitter thing if he were forced out of it and into accepting the second-best.

She tried to remember what her father had told her of Dave Harmon, then Lieutenant Dave Harmon. All she could remember was that he had been furious when Harmon had been transferred from his command. She could remember her father discussing it with her mother, claiming that he would disapprove the transfer himself, and question the wisdom of it all the way to Washington if need be. It had been her mother who had pointed out that the transfer to a regiment known to be ill-officered would doubtless lead to promotion and opportunities for Harmon, and her mother's opinion prevailed. Last night had showed her why her father had been so reluctant to lose Harmon as a junior officer.

The thought now of meeting her parents again almost brought tears to Juliana's eyes. Her mother had written on first coming to Fort Whipple that it was the nicest post they had served on. Its mountain coolness, surrounded by sunblasted deserts, was heaven. The climate was reflected in the actions of everyone on the post and in the pleasant charm of Prescott nearby. Juliana, her mother wrote, would love the place. *If I reach it,* something in the back of her mind whispered.

She straightened up. Why shouldn't she? A gang of roughs had attacked them and had been defeated. What was there to fear?

Sometime before noon the train reached Layton's stage station, which consisted of a mean two-room adobe building and a big stone corral under spreading cottonwoods. The well stood by the corrals, and one of the cottonwoods had been felled and hollowed out to

make a long wide trough that lay against the wall of the
well. Two tall slabs of rock were upended against the
wall of the well and notches had been drilled in the
tips of the slabs to accommodate a log windlass on
which a long length of rope was wound. One end of
the rope was stretched down into the well, while the
other end was attached to the saddle horn of a riderless
pony.

Layton's hostler was already at work; he was a
dirty, middle-aged man in a frayed shirt and cotton
home-made trousers. Now he gave the pony a slap
on the rump and the pony slowly moved off as the
windlass turned and drew up an oaken barrel. The
hostler shouted to his pony to halt, then pulled the barrel onto the wall and tipped its contents into the huge
trough. When the first of Dave's teams were unhooked
and led to water, the trough was almost full.

At the trough Dave stripped off his shirt, ducked
his head in the trough, soaked his shirt, and then put
it back on. When his own teams were watered and
hooked up again, Dave went back to the hostler.

"Can you top off my water barrels for me, Uncle
Ben? We'll have a long haul this afternoon."

"Sure thing," the hostler replied.

As Dave passed his own wagon he lifted the lid of
the oak barrel ironed to the side of his wagon. It was
close to empty, he noted, and he made a mental note
to check the barrel on the other wagons before taking
off. Afterwards he moved into the comparative coolness
and darkness of the stage station.

The common room was a small one holding two
trestle tables; Juliana, Thornton, and Overman were
already seated at one of them. The other table was
filled with the teamsters and troopers, who had taken
care of their horses first. There was, Dave noticed,
no place to sit except at the other table and the only
empty space was beside Juliana Frost. Hanging his hat
on the wall nail, Dave slid onto the bench beside the girl.

From his place he could see through the door into
the outside kitchen, where there was only a stove and
a table under four posts roofed by peeled cottonwood
poles. An Indian woman, Layton's wife, was dishing

food onto tin plates held by Layton's fourteen-year-old
half-breed daughter, whom the teamsters knew as Sissie.
She was small, clean, and cheerful, and was dressed in
only a formless cotton shift. She had the good manners
to put the big bowl of dried beef in cream gravy first
before Juliana.

"Where's your Pa, Sissie?" Dave asked.

"Out looking over your wagons," Sissie said shyly.

Thornton said, "Layton wanted some supplies. No
sense in hauling this grub past his door when it will
just have to be freighted back to him."

Dave said nothing.

"Don't you approve?" Juliana asked, almost sharply.

"I do if my men don't have to unload the wagons,"
Dave said mildly.

Thornton sat up straighter. "Look here, Harmon.
Those goods were consigned to Edwards. We bought
Edwards out and I'll do anything I want with them!"

Dave looked up at him levelly. "Then you'll unload them, too."

Thornton flushed. "That's part of your freighting
job."

"My freighting job ends when these wagons are
pulled up to your warehouse, Thornton. Read your contract." Thornton's face got redder, and he was about to
speak when Dave said mildly, "Sometimes my teamsters pick up some extra money by helping Edwards
unload. It's up to them."

Thornton nodded coldly, and as the beef was
passed he helped himself. Perhaps to relieve the ten-
sion, Lieutenant Overman pointed to Juliana's plate
and said, "Miss Juliana, you'll never get through the
day on that little dab of food."

"I think this heat has killed my appetite." She
looked over at the table where the teamsters and troopers were shoveling down food. "Apparently it hasn't for
anybody else."

Dave said, "Dick is right, Miss Juliana. We won't
reach the next water until about dark."

Juliana gave a half laugh and said resignedly, "All
right then, pass back the platter."

She helped herself to more of the beef and Dave watched her with a sidelong glance. She looked tired and was tired, he knew. Now she passed the food to Dave, who filled his plate, loaded on some bread, poured coffee into his tin cup, and then rose. He was picking up his plate and coffee when Juliana said, "You don't like our company, Dave?"

"No, this is for my hurt teamster," Dave answered.

Thornton, who had been driving the supply wagon, looked surprised and then embarrassed. He had driven with the hurt man all morning and talked with him most of it, and yet he had somehow managed to forget that the man might be hungry. As Dave turned and went out with the food, Thornton gave him a look that held cold fury.

The supply wagon was pulled up in the shade of the cottonwoods, and Everts was half reclining against the side.

"Thought we'd forgotten you, Rich?" Dave asked.

Everts grinned. "I figured no work no eats." He accepted the food thankfully and began eating.

Dave glanced over at one of the wagons and saw old Pappa-Jack Layton and his hostler wrestling out a barrel of flour from the cargo. Cases of food and a keg of horseshoe nails were on the ground beside Layton. Pappa-Jack Layton was a spare, dry man in his sixties whose white beard reached below his Adam's apple. He had, Dave knew, fought more Indians from this place than many a senior cavalry officer had ever seen.

Now a movement out on the desert beyond Layton attracted Dave's attention. He made out a single rider in the distance approaching the station from the south.

Going over to Layton, Dave said, "You've got a visitor coming, Pappa-Jack."

Without even turning to look, Layton said, "I seen him. He ain't used up quite all his luck, has he?"

In ten minutes the visitor, Kirby, leading a pack horse, rode into the shade, reined in, and nodded. To Dave he said, "You Mister Layton?"

Dave gestured with his thumb to Pappa-Jack, meanwhile regarding Kirby, who was looking around him at the loaded wagons. Kirby said, "I rode over to see if you can spare some grub. Kind of looks like you might could."

Pappa-Jack gave a snort of laughter. "Yes, sir. Which wagonload do you want?"

Kirby grinned and dismounted, and now Pappa-Jack's curiosity got the better of his good manners. "Where in tarnation did you come from?"

Kirby tilted his head toward the distant mountains to the south. "Me and a couple of other fellows been prospecting over yonder."

"Where?" Pappa-Jack asked.

Kirby shook his head. "Mister, I can take you there, but I don't know the name of nothing around here, not even the mountains. They told me about your place, though, so when we run out of grub I headed for here."

"You're in the Harquahala Mountains. Found anything?" Pappa-Jack asked.

"Not till day before yesterday," Kirby answered. "We was about to go back when we run into this color. Looks like we might have something. Leastways if we can get some grub we'll stay and see."

While they were talking Dave listened and watched Kirby, assessing the man's story. The troopers, among them Sergeant Noonan, had drifted over, curious as to the identity of the visitor.

"See any Injun sign?" the trooper standing beside Noonan asked.

Kirby regarded the trooper and did not even bother to look at Noonan. "Some, all old though," Kirby said.

Then Dave said, "How come you picked those particular mountains?" There was no challenge in his voice, only curiosity.

"I didn't," Kirby said mildly. "One of my partners did. He used to work in the placers at La Paz. When he saved up enough money he'd project around the country. He always figured there was ore there, so that's why we come back."

It was conceivable to Dave that three men, leaning heavily on luck and caution, and not moving around, could avoid being seen by the Apaches. Still, a man would have to be either foolhardy or very brave to stay on for long.

Now Pappa-Jack said, "What you using for water, mister?"

"We found some, enough to keep us and the horses alive. It ain't good, but you can choke it down."

Pappa-Jack said drily, "If you've found water, don't hang around it long. Them Injuns'll smell it out. Now, what sort of grub you want?"

As Kirby countered with, "What you got?" Dave turned and went back to Everts. As he took Everts' plate and cup he glanced back at Kirby. He seemed in pleasant conversation with Sergeant Noonan. Dave did not give it another thought.

Dave entered the stage station through the outdoor kitchen, where he left Everts' plate with Sissie and received his own food. Going into the eating room, he saw that the troopers and teamsters had finished and that their table was empty. Thornton and Juliana were in conversation at the other table. Dave put his plate down on the teamsters' table, slacked onto the bench, and began eating. In a few moments Thornton, who was smoking a cigar, got up and went out. After his exit, Juliana came over to Dave's table and sat down on the bench opposite him.

"How is the hurt man?" she asked.

"I didn't look at his wound. I figured I wouldn't spoil your work. But he ate all I brought him, so I don't reckon he has a fever."

Juliana hesitated a moment. "I'm ashamed that none of us remembered him," she said.

Dave's loaded fork paused in midair. "Why, he's my responsibility, not yours or Overman's or Thornton's. You doctored him and the Army's transporting him. Seems as if I should see he's fed."

Juliana hesitated a moment as if debating with herself the wisdom of saying what she wanted to say. Then she blurted out, "You don't like John, do you?"

Dave chewed thoughtfully and swallowed. "I don't feel one way or the other about him."

"But I'd think you would," Juliana insisted.

Dave scowled. "Why is that?"

"Because he'll be a good customer of yours in the future. Isn't it just plain good business to accommodate him? Couldn't you have asked a couple of your men to help Mister Layton unload?"

"Is that what Thornton said to you?" Dave asked drily.

Juliana's glance fell away from his. He could see the color mount in her face.

"Well—yes, as a matter of fact. He thinks you embarrassed him unnecessarily. I don't think he'll be anxious to give you his business."

"I think he will, as soon as he's tried some of the other outfits."

"You're best, you mean?" It was Juliana's turn to use a dry manner of speaking.

"I am," Dave said calmly. "My teamsters don't steal and I keep them reasonably sober."

"That's rare in your business?"

"Very rare. Edwards learned how rare it is, and Thornton will learn too."

"But can you afford to lose John's business?"

Dave smiled. "I haven't lost it yet, Miss Juliana; and if I do, it will be my decision, not his."

Juliana eyed him levelly. "You make it sound as if John is working for you rather than you for him."

Dave drank the last of his coffee and put down his cup. "In a way he is," Dave said mildly. "I can leave his goods in my warehouse until they rot. I can have all my wagons out for a month at a time. It's my decision whether Thornton gets his goods promptly, or even gets them at all." He paused, seeking an analogy. "It's the same sort of decision that the captain of the *Sprite* could have made on his last trip. If he chose to put in at Valparaiso for a cargo of hides he could have done it. If I choose to believe that the sutler's store at Camp Grant needs goods ahead of the sutler's store at Whipple, it's my decision."

He rose, drew a silver dollar from his pocket, and laid it on the table. "You can tell Thornton that if you like, Miss Juliana. It may save me from having to tell him."

Juliana Frost said quietly, almost with dislike, "I think you're arrogant."

Dave nodded. "When I have to be, yes."

"What happened last night?" Kirby was asking Sergeant Noonan.

"You took the words out of my mouth," Noonan said drily.

"There was a mounted rider in that herd. He killed Hallam and drove off Schultz. They were to drive off the horses once they were broke loose."

"That was Harmon's doing," Noonan said. "I'll take care of him later. Where are the boys?"

Kirby tilted his head to the south. "Out of sight."

"You got my message, didn't you?"

Kirby nodded.

"There's a batch of big *malpais* this side of King's Wells. You can fort up in that rock. Just don't let them get to water, Kirby. They can't make a fight of it if you stay scattered."

Kirby only nodded again.

"If they can't make it through to water, sooner or later they'll try to come back here. Just don't let them," Noonan said.

"What about that girl?"

"She'll likely bed down in the ambulance, so don't shoot it up. Buy plenty of grub, Kirby. This may take time."

They both fell silent as Pappa-Jack Layton came over. "Want to pick through this stuff, mister?"

4

Troopers Reardon and Adams had instructions from Lieutenant Miller to travel by night and sleep by day. After the first day of the shadeless blasting heat, both men knew it wouldn't work. They dare not try to sleep with their faces uncovered. If they tried to cover them with their blouses, they were close to suffocation. Both men knew that if they were to survive they must travel by day so they could get some sleep at night.

Since the one drink Reardon had taken on the night they had left camp, the older trooper had been abstemious. But by the middle of this day a series of events had driven Reardon to desperation. To begin with, he had spent a near sleepless night stretched out on the rocky desert floor. His feet were already blistered and his bones ached with the unaccustomed chore of walking all day in the blasting sun. The heat today had seemed to dry out his body, and a dozen times in the night he had roused for a drink of water.

Thus, at the beginning of this day's march Reardon was tired, still thirsty, sore-footed, and surly. An hour out of their camp he was stumbling with Adams along the edge of some hardpan which held scant vegetation. Reardon was paying no attention to what was underfoot, so that it was too late when he heard the rattle. The snake struck at his leg just above the boot top. It was Adams who killed the snake while Reardon, in panic, stripped down his trousers to see what the snake's bite had done. He could see that the marks of the fangs had barely broken the skin. Was it serious enough to bother with or not? Trooper Adams thought it was. Reardon wasn't sure, but he couldn't afford to take the chance that it wasn't.

Accordingly, Reardon ordered Adams to slash the flesh where the fangs had broken it. Adams, nauseated at the thought of having to cut into human flesh, was even more afraid of not doing a thorough job. He cut deeply and painfully into Reardon's leg, then sucked at the gushing blood of the wound as Reardon directed him. The trouble was the wound was too deep and it bled freely for half an hour before they could check it. Once the blood stopped flowing, Adams, again on Reardon's orders, hacked off Reardon's shirt tail with his knife and made a crude bandage.

It was then that Reardon thought of the whiskey. Everyone, including Trooper Adams, knew that whiskey was the ancient antidote for snakebite.

In the broiling sun then Reardon gulped down a generous portion of the raw, blood-warm whiskey, following it with a minute gulp of water. He did not want to dilute the sheer pleasure of the raw whiskey churning in his belly.

Hauled to his feet by Adams, he tried walking. Not only did his swollen feet hurt now, but his leg ached and throbbed with every movement. Still he had no choice but to slog onward. Behind his pain, of course, were unanswered questions. Had Adams doctored the bite in time? How long did it take for the venom to work? How did a man die of snake bite? After fifteen minutes pondering these questions Reardon took stock of his state of physical and mental health, found them both bad, halted, and took another drink of whiskey. He observed Trooper Adams watching him dispassionately in the blinding heat.

After gaggind down the warm whiskey and catching his breath, Reardon said, "That eases it a little, sonny."

"If it does, then you'd better save it for later," Adams said. There was nothing save disapproval in his tone—no force, no attempt to dominate the situation, and no pity. He had spoken as if to record his disapproval with his conscience.

Reardon knew that his wound had slowed their pace to a crawl, but whiskey made him indifferent to the fact. He was doing the best he could and the whiskey helped. He could feel the slow ooze of blood down into his boot, and still it did not greatly concern him. He was simply doing the best he could.

All through the morning at their hourly stops Trooper Adams would gnaw on a piece of bread or bacon, then lie flat out with his hat over his face as if he were gathering strength from the earth. At each of these stops Trooper Reardon, eating nothing, had another drink of whiskey. By midday he was drunk and hurting.

It was at one of these stops that Trooper Adams, again sprawled out, lifted his hat off his face to regard Reardon, who had just finished a drink. Even sitting down, Reardon swayed as he muttered to himself something that was unintelligible to Adams. It was then the thought came to Trooper Adams: *I'm going to have to leave him.* But when and how? With food and water? What good would they do, Trooper Adams thought coldly. With both of them moving toward help perhaps they had enough food and water, but if they stayed in one place waiting for Trooper Reardon to sober up and his leg to heal, they would surely die. This afternoon would tell whether Reardon could pull himself together, stop his drinking, and labor on, or whether he would simply give up.

It was an afternoon of exquisite hell for Trooper Adams. He not only had the memory of the snake incident with its possible aftermath riding him, but he had to come to some decision about Reardon. The older man now that he could openly claim his drinking was medicinal, managed to put away more than half the contents of his whiskey canteen. The oven-hot sunlight was hard enough for Trooper Adams to bear, but Trooper Reardon's drunken reactions to it were almost unbearable to watch. He was, Trooper Adams knew, in a kind of crazy delirium. He kept imagining they were approaching Camp McDowell, and apparently he could see it in his mind. For once, in spite of his condition, he started to run with great staggering, lurching steps until he fell to the desert floor. At times he knew Trooper Adams, and at other times he would ask Adams his name, as if he had no memory of him.

At their hourly rest period Reardon went to sleep and Trooper Adams used up fifteen minutes slapping him, punching him, and pinching him before he would open his eyes. It was probably a combination of drink and heat that caused it, but his broad face had turned an alarming shade of flaming red. Trooper Adams had no idea whether this resulted from drink or from the remains of the snake venom, and as he hauled Reardon to his feet, he knew real despair. They had made only half a mile in the last hour and now Reardon could scarcely stand upright.

Backing away from him, Trooper Adams said coldly, "Get going, Reardon."

Reardon looked at him blankly. "Where we going?"

For answer, Adams only lifted his arm and pointed north.

Reardon lurched into motion and then his legs collapsed. He fell on his knees among the low mesquite and stared at the ground. Trooper Adams came over to him and stood before him, hands on hips.

"Get up or I'll leave you, Reardon," he said in an almost gentle voice.

Reardon appeared not to hear him. He hoarsely mumbled something that Adams could not make out. Adams now went up to him, knelt before him, put a hand on either shoulder, and shook the older man savagely. Reardon's head rolled loosely and his hat fell off. Adams retrieved it, slapped it on Reardon's head and then, still kneeling, said angrily, "Do you understand me? I'm leaving. Come along if you want."

The shaking seemed to have brought Reardon to his senses, and he shook his head as if rousing from a dream and looked at Adams with blood-shot eyes. "Don't leave me," he whispered.

Then Trooper Adams' temper really flared. "You damned drunk!" he said savagely. "You're killing us both! Our water's almost gone. So's our food. The men are depending on us, and here you are in the middle of nowhere so drunk you can't walk."

Reardon shook his head again. "Let me sleep it off, sonny."

"You'll die!" Adams yelled at him. "Pour your booze on the ground. Then walk it off or I'll leave you!"

Sweat, both from heat and from fever, was pouring down Reardon's face, but his hand clamped protectively over the canteen. As Adams watched him, Reardon's eyes glazed over and he toppled over on his side. Adams looked at him for a long moment in helpless wrath. How far did his obligation to a fellow human being go? It wasn't Reardon's fault that the snake had bitten him, that his leg had been cut, but neither was it Adams' fault. It was clearly Reardon's fault that he now lay in a drunken stupor and probably would lie in one for the rest of the day and night, and start in again tomorrow. Only the Lord knew if, when he awakened, he would be too sick to move.

Trooper Adams' shrewd instinct for survival spoke to him now. *What do I owe him?* he thought. *My life?* Although he had told Reardon that ten men's lives depended on him, this fact did not figure in his decision now. He was going to stay alive if brains, courage, and endurance could stave off death. Nobody, least of all a sodden trooper, was going to interfere with that. He would leave Reardon with the food and drink that he was carrying. If Reardon could survive, well and good. If he couldn't, Adams was not going to die with him.

Trooper Adams got to his feet, toed Reardon roughly with his boot, and said harshly, "I'm going."

Reardon didn't answer. On an impulse Adams couldn't explain, he reached down, picked up Reardon's hat and put it over his face; then he turned and started north.

He had walked perhaps fifteen yards when an alien sound caused him to halt and turn to look back at Reardon. What he saw was Reardon's pistol cocked and pointed at him.

Trooper Adams simply fell to the ground in the low greasewood as Reardon's gun went off. Adams was clawing open the holster of his own gun when a searching shot close to him whistled through the mesquite. Pulling out his gun and rolling over on his belly, he peered through the sparse brush and made out the outline of Reardon's body. He sighted carefully and pulled the trigger. An awful grunt following told him that he had hit Reardon.

He lay there for an interminable minute, then rose and cautiously made his way to where Reardon lay. He halted, saw that his bullet had caught Reardon in the chest and that he was unmistakably dead.

Trooper Adams, in a kind of trance, stared at the body, examining his own feelings. He had killed Reardon in self-defense, but who would believe him? Then the thing to do when he reached help was to say that Trooper Reardon had died of a sunstroke. Coldly now,

Adams calculated on the best way to dispose of Reardon's body. He couldn't bury it, and there were no rocks around to pile upon it. What did it matter, he wondered. What did he owe to Reardon's memory? Nothing. The man had tried to kill him.

Trying not to look at Reardon's face, Adams slipped the two remaining canteens off Reardon's body and over his own, and took Reardon's bread and bacon. Then he set out north, a calm and resolute young man who had survived again. Only once did he look back, and he saw the vultures overhead sweeping in long descending spirals before their rendezvous with Reardon.

Reardon and Adams hadn't been gone from camp a day before Lieutenant Miller realized that something would have to be done to keep up the morale of his men. Their ordinary chores, such as mounted drill, keeping their horses groomed and their equipment in shape—in fact all the duties and occupations of a trooper—were lacking, since the reasons for doing them were gone. Cooking assignments were negligible. Policing the camp took fifteen minutes. When the latrines were dug, that ended the duties. The men contrived to manufacture some shade with their ground sheets and blankets and simply lay listlessly under them on the supply wagon through the blazing day.

That evening Lieutenant Miller called Corporal Chasen over to his tent, which was out of earshot of the other seven men. Chasen saluted and Lieutenant Miller said, "At ease, Corporal. Sit down."

Chasen obeyed, although reluctantly. When Lieutenant Miller was standing, Corporal Chasen towered over him and it gave him a psychological advantage that bred confidence. Seated, he lost this advantage.

"Notice the men today, Corporal?"

"Notice how, sir?"

"Once the camp was cleaned up, they just drowsed in the shade, playing cards, talking, and sleeping."

Corporal Chasen frowned. "There isn't much else they can do, Mister Miller." Usually Chasen addressed Lieutenant Miller as Lieutenant, a subtle form of flattery since only a first lieutenant was entitled to be addressed as one. A second lieutenant was normally addressed as "mister."

Chasen's form of address now did not escape Lieutenant Miller, and it irritated him. "If there's nothing else to do, we'll make something else. We may be here ten more days, Corporal. I'm not going to have men under my command sleeping or yarning the day through."

"What did you have in mind, sir?" There was a wariness, almost dread, in Chasen's tone of voice.

"Tomorrow you'll take out a search detail of three men, Corporal. I want you to circle the camp, always keeping it in sight, but just barely. The other two men will just barely keep you and each other in sight."

"And what are we searching for, sir?"

"Rocks."

Corporal Chasen was quiet a moment, then asked slowly, "What do we do with the rocks, sir?"

Lieutenant Miller ignored this. "When any of you find a suitable amount of rock, you're to return to camp."

"With the rock, sir?"

"A sample. The rock has to be the size that a man can carry."

Corporal Chasen nodded and asked, "What will the rock be for, sir?"

Lieutenant Miller evaded the answer again. "While you're searching, I'll have the remaining three men digging out this seep. The rock is to wall it up and make a well."

Corporal Chasen frowned. "We're getting more than enough water now, sir, especially with the horses and two men gone."

Lieutenant Miller's normally aggressive features settled into even more aggressive lines. "Corporal, you've had the point explained to you and have missed it. I want to keep my men active and in good condition. I want them exercising their muscles. You understand that now?"

"I understand, sir."

Lieutenant Miller continued. "If we have the well

finished before help arrives, then we'll build a stone corral, even if it's to hold horses for only one night. These men will be kept busy every waking hour. You understand that, Corporal?"

Corporal Chasen nodded. "It'll be murdering work in this heat, sir."

"But work it will be. That's all that will save the sanity of these men—work." He paused. "Choose the men you want to take along with you, and start as soon as there's enough light to see by."

Corporal Chasen assembled the six men, who squatted in the shade of two ground sheets tied together while they listened to him.

It was fat Wilson, from under whose nose the Apaches had stolen their horses, who spoke first, and angrily. "What in hell does he want this seep rocked up for? It ain't on any road or trail and never will be."

"It's just made work," another man said angrily.

Corporal Chasen answered him mildly. "It's meant to be, boys. It's meant to be. You're all getting soft and you're idle, says the lieutenant."

There was a muttered obscenity from Wilson about what the lieutenant and all officers could do, and Chasen blandly agreed. Then he said, "Wilson, you'll come with me along with Ryan. The rest of you will stay here and dig out the seep and take turns cooking."

Next morning Chasen, Ryan, and Wilson, heavily armed, set out on the search for suitable rock, while the remaining three men began excavating the seep with their mess tins. Lieutenant Miller read and slept while the excavators muttered curses and obscenities. To all six men this job was a senseless cruelty. It was as if they had been ordered to build a twenty-foot-high castle out of sand on some remote beach just so it could be washed away by the next tide.

If Miller had put it squarely to them that this was a game to keep their hands and minds occupied and had then joined in the game himself, they might have gone along grudgingly. But to hear their officer snoring in the tent while they labored under the blazing sun in their sweat-drenched uniforms was almost intolerable.

At their midday break for food the lieutenant was awake but aloof. He never left the shade of his tent. An hour later, when Chasen and his sweat-drenched search party trudged into camp, Chasen had to rouse Lieutenant Miller.

"Sir, we found the rock." He tossed a melon-sized piece of rock at Miller's feet.

Lieutenant Miller yawned. "How far away, Corporal?"

"We figured about two miles, sir."

"Good." Lieutenant Miller's face expressed real pleasure. "How do you propose to transport the rock, Corporal?"

"I hadn't thought of it, sir," Chasen said sullenly.

"Well, think about it now."

"The horse packs we brought in the wagon?" Chasen asked.

Miller nodded. "And slung over a rifle, a man at each end."

"Two men couldn't lift a pack full of stones."

"Then carry as much as you can. Get something to eat before you start out, Corporal."

Corporal Chasen and Troopers Wilson and Ryan had the usual noon meal of bread, bacon, and dried apples that were tough as a mule's ear in spite of their soaking. The excavating crew were already at work again in the blazing sun tearing rock off the pit. While he was chewing stoically, Corporal Chasen, even though slow of wit, made an observation.

He had his noon smoke, rose, and went over to Lieutenant Miller's tent. Miller, stripped to the waist and sweating, was sitting cross-legged, writing his daily report. At Chasen's approach he paused and waited for Chasen to speak.

"Sir, I've just had an idea," Chasen said.

"Tell me."

"We're digging enough rock out of that seep to wall it," Chasen said.

Lieutenant Miller looked at him pityingly and then gave a soft groan. "You still don't understand, Corporal. Maybe we could use those rocks and have the seep walled up by night. What would the men do tomorrow?"

Chasen said with a touch of surliness in his voice, "After the day they'll have put in, I reckon they'll rest tomorrow."

"They'll rest during the night, Corporal," Miller said tartly.

Corporal Chasen regarded him in a long and barely respectful silence, then he said, "Another thing, sir. Three men hauling rocks doesn't make any sense. If you want rocks you should detail one more man to haul them. It'll take two to a pack. Or if you want the well dug deeper, you should take a man off a hauling detail and put him on the digging."

Lieutenant Miller pondered this a minute, then smiled faintly and said, "Good idea, Corporal. Take Schermer off the digging detail and put him on the hauling."

"Yes, sir." Corporal Chasen saluted and went back toward his men. He was seething with anger, but he was too good a soldier to let it show in his face. Curtly he summoned the German-born Schermer to join them. After sorting out two of the stoutest, newest horse packs, or *aparejos,* which were simply two large canvas pouches joined together that could be thrown over a horse's back if the country got too rough for a wagon, the detail set out across the desert. The whole flat, seemingly endless, blazing landscape shimmered in the sun, and it was only Corporal Chasen's tracking that guided them to the rock bar thrust up just above the floor of the desert. When they reached the rock bar and fell exhausted to the ground, they found the rocks so hot they could not lie on them. There was nothing to do but load as quickly as possible and get back to camp. The handling of the rocks was a minor torture, for they were so hot that they could be held only for a second or so before the heat burned through their gauntlets.

The first mile of their return they found that both pairs of men had been over-optimistic about the load they could pack and consequently they jettisoned a part of their load. By the time they reached camp and unloaded they were dizzy and sick from their labor. They rested a few minutes in the shade and then, goaded by Lieutenant Miller's silent surveillance, they set off again.

When it came time for the evening meal, every man in camp save Lieutenant Miller was too tired to eat. They lay on the ground drained of all energy, too exhausted to argue or even to talk. When blessed darkness came, they rolled into their blankets.

To a man, they watched Lieutenant Miller's small tent. He had directed the cooks to save their bacon drippings, and out of them, by twisting a short length of rope into a wick in a tin cup, he had made himself a lamp of sorts. His was the only light save the stars, and the only sounds were the exhausted snoring and the measured tread of the weary sentries. Chasen, watching the light, hated Lieutenant Miller as he had never hated a man before.

"Corporal." He heard this whispered behind him, rolled over, and saw that Wilson had thrown his blanket down beside him. Chasen was still unforgiving toward this thick-set, cynical, and aggressive trooper who had spent a third of the time since Chasen had known him in the guardhouse or doing punishment for insubordination. Chasen's grunt of acknowledgment held no welcome.

Now Wilson whispered, "The lieutenant's gone crazy."

"He don't think so," Chasen whispered back.

"We going to do this tomorrow?"

"So he said."

"I got blisters on my feet a half-inch high."

"Cut off your shirttail and make bandages out of it," Chasen whispered angrily. His own calloused feet were sore to the point of blistering.

"If we got to do this, why don't we do it at night?"

Chasen's double-word answer, "The lieutenant," brought a grunt of disdain from Wilson.

"By God, I'm going to report him," Wilson said.

"You better hope you got grounds," Chasen muttered.

There was a long silence and then Wilson spoke again. "I'm reporting sick tomorrow."

"Go ahead. See where it gets you."

"By God, I will!" Wilson whispered vehemently. "They can't do this to a man!"

"Where have I heard that before? Now shut up," Chasen said.

Next morning Wilson was not allowed by Miller to report on sick call, and the same torturous day began. As punishment to Wilson for dogging it, Corporal Chasen and Schermer were allowed to change places with the digging detail. Wilson and Ryan were kept on the rock detail.

The only variation from the routine of the previous day was that Lieutenant Miller made a visit to the rock bar. Here in the furnace heat he watched the men gingerly load the fire-hot rocks into the *aparejos*. After yesterday's experience, each of the rock-hauling crew had cut out a couple of swatches from their blankets and used them as pads over their gauntlets to shield their flesh when they picked up the rocks. However, bandages couldn't help Wilson's feet; his blisters had broken and his soles were cracked and bleeding. Observing Wilson's painful hobble, Lieutenant Miller only commented cheerfully, "They'll soon toughen up, Wilson."

Wilson did not bother to answer, and Lieutenant Miller, apparently satisfied that his troopers were working, returned to camp, stripped again, and went to sleep. That evening at supper the men were more exhausted than they had been the night before, and Corporal Chasen had to warn them that however tired they were they must eat to keep up their strength.

After they had eaten, Corporal Chasen put a pinch of tobacco that he was hoarding carefully into his pipe, lighted it, and then contemplated the camp. There was a mound of gravel and rock beside the seep, which was now excavated to a depth of five feet. Beside this mound was another mound of rock, higher and broader. The useless labor represented there sickened Chasen and he wondered how much taller the mounds would grow. Unless help came within the next few days a sizable piece of desert real estate would have been transported two miles for no reason at all. The only good that had come of digging out the seep was that they now had more water—more than they could use.

"Corporal Chasen!" It was Lieutenant Miller's voice, and Chasen rose and made his way toward Miller's tent. As he passed the tarpaulins he saw that the two men who had drawn early morning guard duty were deep in the sleep of exhaustion. Wilson, now that the sun was almost down, was sitting off by himself, moodily contemplating the vast reach of desert before him. His wrists were on his knees and his hands hung down from them like two chunks of tender meat. It seemed odd to Chasen that only Wilson's feet had blistered so badly; then he remembered that for many months Wilson had been the quartermaster's clerk and his only job was to sit at a desk and count and make a note of supplies issued.

Corporal Chasen halted before the tent and saluted languidly. "Yes, sir."

Lieutenant Miller had been reading his report book and now he looked up. "Corporal, I went over our remaining rations today. I think we'd better cut down."

"They're pretty thin now, sir, for men doing hard work. If we cut down on rations, we'll have to cut down on the work, sir."

"Have to?" Miller's tone was cutting. "Are you giving orders, Corporal?"

Chasen felt his face go hot. "I meant to say we should cut down, sir."

"That's better," Lieutenant Miller said. He thought a moment. "We can alternate the rock detail with the digging detail. Digging is easier, I gather."

The corporal only nodded.

Miller continued, "All except for Wilson. He stays on the rock detail. That's all, Corporal."

Afterward, to the men who were still awake, Chasen imparted the news of half rations and alternating details. The men heard him out listlessly, too apathetic from exhaustion to protest. He looked at Wilson, who had now joined the others. He was sitting down and each blistered bare foot was cradled on the opposite thigh.

"All except you, Wilson. The lieutenant said you're to stay on the rock detail."

"You didn't have to tell me," Wilson said, in a strangely quiet voice. "I knew it already."

The sentries were put out before darkness came, and afterward the rest of the men turned in. Corporal Chasen chose a spot away from Wilson tonight, for he didn't want to be kept awake by Wilson's grousing. Again Lieutenant Miller was writing in his tent by the light of his home-made lamp. Watching him, Chasen was seized by a sudden depression. Would it be possible, when they were rescued, to report Miller's senseless cruelty? His enlisted man's wisdom told him no. For that matter, would they ever be rescued? There was no guarantee that Reardon and Adams would reach help. Maybe they were all spending the last days of their lives here; seven men laboring themselves to death and the eighth man sitting in a tent whiling away his last hours scribbling with the stub of a pencil in a book.

It wasn't exactly scribbling, since Lieutenant Miller wrote a neat and precise hand acquired as the regimental historian at the Presidio. This night he wrote: "Today was uneventful, but I think the men are beginning to respond physically as a result of my well-building project. They are not as sluggish, and they no longer kill time by talk and cards. Tonight I told Corporal Chasen that I had taken an inventory of our remaining supplies and that we would be forced to go on half rations. This was not entirely true, but I did it for two reasons. If rescue does not come within a few more days, I am determined to make a march of it to the north. I want my men to be lean and durable, with not an extra ounce of fat on their bodies. The second reason for putting them on half rations is that we do not know how long our march will be. However long, we cannot make it without sufficient food."

Lieutenant Miller closed his book, rose, and saw that the sentries were circling camp; then he extinguished his lamp, lay down, and slept.

Next morning at bare dawn the sentry awakened Corporal Chasen, who roused the men. Since the surrounding dry and sparse mesquite had been exhausted for fuel, they were now breaking up the pack frames for fuel for their one fire a day. Pan bread had to be baked and bacon fried to last the detail until the following morning.

The camp stirred with activity. Some of the men washed with water poured from canteens, while others filled their canteens from the well whose muddy water had settled during the night. Corporal Chasen eyed Lieutenant Miller's tent and saw that the lieutenant was still asleep. He did not understand how a man could sleep most of the day, and all night through the dawn. He had to concede, however, that usually Lieutenant Miller was up with his men. Perhaps he had stayed awake late into the night writing in his book.

However, when the food was ready Corporal Chasen walked over to the low tent and said loudly, "Morning, sir. Food's ready, sir."

There was no answer.

Corporal Chasen knelt down and looked into the tent. Lieutenant Miller, stripped to the waist, lay on his face. Chasen's hand was moving to shake his shoulder when he saw the blood on Lieutenant Miller's back. From a knife wound in the back the blood had flowed down the lieutenant's side and had pooled on his bankket before leaving a wide dark stain.

For a stunned moment Chasen stared at the wound, then reached out and touched Lieutenant Miller's shoulder. The flesh was cold. The corporal snatched his hand back, then he rose, turned, and bellowed, "Over here, on the double!" The men looked at him a moment and then came running.

To the first man who arrived, Schermer, the corporal said, "Take a corner of that blanket and help me haul him out."

Schermer and Chasen, each on a corner of the blanket, pulled the body of Lieutenant Miller out into view where the assembling troopers could see him.

Watching their faces, the corporal saw many emotions reflected. The younger troopers stared at the body with a kind of fascinated horror. The older troopers looked indifferent, almost relieved. It was Ryan who first found his tongue. "Apaches?"

The corporal addressed himself to the sentries on the first watch. "Either of you know anything about this? Did you see anything or hear anything?"

Both men shook their heads.

Chasen asked the same question of the two troopers who had relieved them, and received the same answer. One of them added, "It was moonlight when we took over. We'd have seen anything that moved."

Slowly, Corporal Chasen looked into the face of each man. There had not yet been a single expression of regret or pity from any one of them, and Chasen was an old enough soldier to know why. Miller had bred no loyalty, only abiding hatreds. The corporal was sure, in his own mind, that one of the detail had murdered Lieutenant Miller.

Chasen said abruptly, "Let me see your knives."

Each man in the detail had a different sort of knife; they ranged from pocket knives to hunting knives. Obediently the men extended them, and as Corporal Chasen made a slow circle he examined each knife for bloodstains. When he came to Wilson, the sullen trooper held out a hunting knife in his palm. It was as clean as the rest.

This was foolish, Corporal Chasen concluded. To destroy evidence all a man would have to do would be to wash off his knife with water from his canteen.

Again Corporal Chasen looked at each man individually, and each met his eye with an expression of indifference that could have been a normal expression of innocence. He looked longest at Wilson and saw nothing in the man's cold stare that hadn't been there before.

Chasen said heavily, "It looks like my rank says I take command." He paused. "Anybody feel like arguing it?"

"You've got the only rank in the bunch of us," Ryan said. "Looks like you got to take command."

When the others nodded, Chasen said, "Then I'll give my first one. Go eat."

The men drifted away to their small fire, but Chasen remained. Out of some obscure sense of propriety he knelt in the opening of the tent, reached for Lieutenant Miller's blouse and covered his upper body and head with it; then he rose, circled the tent, and looked for tracks. There were tracks everywhere, Chasen saw, and there was no possible way of telling their age or identity. He stood and stared at the ground, wondering what he must do with this new responsibility. For the first time in his soldier's career he realized the awesome burden placed on an officer. He, as Lieutenant Miller had been, was responsible for these men's lives.

Half an hour later the whole detail, save for the crippled Wilson, trudged the two miles to the rock bar, Corporal Chasen sometimes leading, sometimes taking his turn carrying the blanket-wrapped body that was slung on another blanket whose sides were stiffened by rolling them around two rifles.

At the rock bar Lieutenant Miller's body was laid on the ground and at Corporal Chasen's orders the men began to pile rocks on it. When the mound was perhaps a yard high, Corporal Chasen called a halt. The men surrounded the grave and at the corporal's orders removed their hats. Then Corporal Chasen, reaching into distant memory, stumbled through the words of the Lord's prayer. Afterwards he signaled for the men to return to camp.

"We work today, Corporal?" one of the detail asked. They were all listening for his answer.

"We rest today," Corporal Chasen replied.

They were scarcely back at camp before Corporal Chasen noted the subtle difference in the attitude of the detail toward him. Now that he was giving orders, the men eyed him warily, and since he had succeeded the commanding officer he lay down in the commanding officer's tent, which was almost as hot as the scalding sunlight outside.

Inevitably his thoughts turned to Lieutenant Miller's murderer. Corporal Chasen knew he was not a bright man, but he thought he should be able to do more than he had to ferret out the lieutenant's killer.

The trouble was there wasn't a man in the detail who didn't have reason to kill Miller. He had abused them all—but especially he had abused Wilson.

Now Corporal Chasen pondered what he knew about Wilson. He doubted very much if Wilson had enlisted under his own name. He was from an eastern city, Chasen judged, because his loud, aggressive cynicism was foreign to country or small-town men. Most troopers, Chasen knew, accepted their chores and assignments with a kind of fatalism, but not Wilson. He maneuvered and bribed among his equals; he fawned upon his superiors when they allowed it, but when they did not his actions verged on insubordination. Fawning had got him his job as quartermaster clerk, where he was excused from many of the chores required of the other troopers. He was derisive of any man wanting to advance himself, and was a gambler of real talent. A man with an extraordinarily lewd mind, Wilson had been a pimp in civilian life, Chasen guessed.

All in all, Chasen could find no virtues in Wilson, and all the vices attributable to a bad soldier. In his own mind he was certain that Wilson had killed the lieutenant. However, there was one more factor that should be weighed. What did his fellow troopers think of Wilson?

He cast back over the roster. Schermer hated Wilson because Wilson never addressed Schermer except as "You block-headed Dutchman." Prince hated him because Wilson consistently cheated at cards and Prince could not discover how he was doing it. As he went down the roster, he could find some reason for every man disliking or fearing Wilson.

Corporal Chasen was slow to make up his mind, but once it was made up he was a man of action. He raised up on an elbow and called, "Wilson, come over here."

All of the troopers had sought shade. Four of them were lying under the supply wagon, and Wilson was one of these.

Now Wilson called back, "Come over here, Corporal. My feet hurt."

Corporal Chasen rose, lifted the flap of his holster,

pulled out his pistol, and strode over to the wagon, halting in front of Wilson.

"I'm commanding this outfit and I give the orders. I gave you an order, Wilson. Obey it." His deceptively pleasant voice held a menace that was not lost on Wilson, but to the fat trooper this was a matter of saving face.

Wilson said, "What you've got to say, you can say to me here, can't you?"

For answer, Corporal Chasen shot into the dirt an inch or so from Wilson's feet. "On your feet, trooper," the corporal said flatly.

Wilson scrambled up on all fours, cleared the wagon, and stood up. "I'll report that, Corporal," Wilson said.

"Do that," Chasen said drily. "Now get over to the tent."

Wilson limped over to the tent with Chasen following him. When he halted, Chasen circled him and surveyed him a long moment, hands on hips.

"You're pullin' rank you ain't got, Corporal. Remember that."

Chasen didn't answer, and Wilson said, "Can I sit down?"

"No." Chasen looked beyond Wilson at the men, who were all watching him. Then his glance settled onto Wilson. He said quietly, "You killed Miller, didn't you?"

Wilson grinned crookedly. "Prove it, Corporal. What are we talking for?"

"For me," Chasen said slowly. "You hated the lieutenant."

"So did you. So did every man here."

"Yes, we all hated him, but you killed him."

"Like I said, prove it."

"I can't," Chasen answered. "Still, I'd like to hear you admit it." He looked around him. "Nobody can hear us, and there were no witnesses. Court-martial can't touch you."

"What are you going to report, Corporal?" Wilson asked slyly.

"Only that Lieutenant Miller was stabbed to death by someone in this detail."

"You're sure you won't say you suspect me?"

Chasen nodded. "If I'm asked, I will; but what evidence has anybody got?"

"None," Wilson said smugly.

"All right, then, did you kill him?" the corporal asked.

Now it was Wilson's turn to look around the camp, making sure nobody but Chasen could hear him. He turned back and smiled crookedly. "Sure, I killed him," he said softly. "It was either him or me. You heard him keep me off the sick call. You saw him give me double work. What was I supposed to do, let him kill me?"

Corporal Chasen said calmly, "No, the lieutenant had it coming. I think he was a little bit crazy. I don't reckon I blame you for killing him, but I blame you for the way you did it."

Wilson laughed soundlessly. "You think I should have pulled a gun on him and shot him where all of you could see it?"

"No. But I don't think you should have stabbed him in the back while he was sleeping."

"And what are you going to do about it?" Wilson asked.

Corporal Chasen's hands were still on his hips. Now he took a half-step forward, then moved with the swiftness of a striking snake; his ham-shaped right fist sledged into Wilson's shelving jaw, which was wet and slippery with perspiration. But the blow was exactly aimed and the sound of it could be heard through the camp. It was the sound of flesh on bone that was being broken. Wilson, caught by surprise, simply fell backwards, unconsciousness coming so swiftly that he did not even attempt to break his fall.

The men who had been watching came to their feet and, looking at each other, moved up to Chasen and Wilson. They ringed the two men, looking alternately at Wilson and then at Chasen.

Finally Prince asked, "Why'd you hit him, Corporal?"

"He'll tell you if he wants; I won't," Chasen said flatly.

One of the men knelt beside Wilson, put a hand on his jaw, and moved it. The jaw gave easily, loosely, as it was moved from side to side, and the unconscious Wilson seemed to have no knowledge of it.

The trooper looked up. "You broke his jaw, Corporal."

Corporal Chasen nodded. "I figured to."

5

Dave knew from past trips that the long haul from Pappa-Jack Layton's place to King's Wells was the hottest and most uncomfortable part of the trip to Whipple. There were stretches of *malpais* and blown sand that required double-teaming, as had been done the first day out of Ehrenburg. This in turn demanded that the escort, the ambulance, with Juliana driving, and the supply wagon, with Thornton at the reins, halt in the broiling afternoon sun. The glare off the sand and rock was close to blinding, especially in the stretches of blow sand.

It was after Dave had bulled the second wagon through a stretch of sand and was returning for the third that he passed the ambulance where Juliana was slacked on the seat. Her hand shaded her closed eyes, but Dave saw that her face was flushed. He handed over the reins of the eight mules to his teamster and walked over to the ambulance, which Juliana had pulled off the road. It was even too hot for visiting, Dave observed, as he saw Thornton limply sprawl out on the seat of the supply wagon.

At Dave's approach Juliana looked up and a faint hostility came into her eyes. Dave pulled down the neckerchief from his face and said, "Miss Juliana, do you have a veil or a big handkerchief in your gear?"

"Why, I think I could find one."

"Then you should tie it across your face. You're getting sunburned."

"But I haven't been in the sun all day," Juliana protested.

"You don't have to be in the sun. The glare off this sand can burn you as badly as direct sunlight."

"Is that why you and your men always have your neckerchiefs over your faces?"

"That, and the dust our teams kick up."

Juliana nodded. "How much longer must we travel today?"

Dave thought a moment and answered, "Till about dark, I'd judge." Then he added, "Don't expect much when we come to King's Wells."

"How do you mean that?"

"There are only a few cottonwoods around a caved-in spring. There's an adobe building, but it's abandoned and full of snakes and scorpions."

"Abandoned?"

"The stage line gave up trying to stock it after they lost three station tenders and all the stock."

"Indians?"

When Dave only nodded, Juliana glanced off at the uneven desert floor that held nothing but greasewood, rock mounds, and cactus. She said softly, "This is a cruel, cruel country, isn't it, Dave?"

"It never lets up on you," Dave agreed.

Juliana gave him a searching glance. "Maybe that explains you," she said quietly.

At that moment Sergeant Noonan rode up and said pleasantly, "They're waiting for you, Mister Harmon."

"Remember the veil," Dave said, and went along. He passed the supply wagon and did not even look at Thornton, nor did Thornton look at him. He saw that Everts, on his pallet of blankets, was sleeping, and then he moved on.

Sergeant Noonan rode up to his side, pulled a foot from his stirrup, and said agreeably, "Climb up behind." Dave accepted his offer and swung up behind him.

"This is a good horse you're riding, Sergeant."

Noonan half turned his head. "I think he is, but I haven't had him out of a slow walk yet."

"Plan to race him? He looks like he could."

"I reckon I might. Prescott's a gambling town."

The horse labored sturdily through the deep, soft sand with his double burden. Noonan then turned his head and, pointing to the sand, said, "You've got something broke in that last wagon that went through. See those spots like coal oil every once in a while?"

"It's those army rifles. They're still draining the packing grease."

Noonan simply said, "Oh, so that's it," in a disinterested voice.

Back at the wagons they spent another idle halfhour while the remaining wagons were double-teamed across the blow sand. Afterwards, when Dave climbed into his saddle and got his team in motion behind the supply wagon, he recalled his conversation with Juliana Frost. In reply to his observation that the country never lets up on you she had said, *Maybe that explains you.* What had she meant by that, he wondered. Was it in reference to their discussion about Thornton and Dave's refusal to give an inch to Thornton's demands? Was she implying that this cruel country had made him cruel, too? He supposed she was, and he wondered if there was more than a grain of truth in her statement. To him Thornton was simply a willful man who threatened to stand in the way of a necessary job. *No, that's not quite honest,* he thought. The truth of the matter was that Thornton merely annoyed him and that, in turn, he had been unnecessarily sharp with him.

Why had he let himself be annoyed? Thornton was merely a soft, undoubtedly sharp trader who lived in a world of ledgers that had no appeal to Dave. Or did his annoyance stem from the fact that Juliana Frost seemed to like Thornton, maybe with a fondness that could be called love? In plainer words, was he jealous of Thornton?

The thought was sobering. If he was jealous of Thornton, maybe that also explained his impatience with Juliana, who seemed to favor Thornton over himself.

For the first time in months Dave made a close examination of himself, and unconsciously raised his gloved hand to touch his eyepatch. Since his accident in the closing days of the war he had accepted the fact that he was something of a freak. Given the choice of two personable men, one with one eye, the other with two, a normal girl would choose the latter, Dave thought. And, believing this, he had not sought out attractive women, nor had he avoided them. He had merely accepted the fact that to an attractive woman, as to the Army, he was somehow flawed. In sum then, he was forced to admit to himself that he was attracted to Juliana Frost, that she was attracted to John Thornton, and that in consequence he was jealous of Thornton and impatient with Juliana. *Now I know,* he thought wryly. *It took me three days to figure it out, but now I know.*

It was late afternoon when the train could see ahead a slight change both in color and shape of the flat horizon. It became irregular, not quite hilly. Instead of the sand-to-gray color of the country they were passing through, there was s shimmering thin line of black which puzzled Lieutenant Overman. He checked his flankers, who were barely in sight, then dropped back from the side of the ambulance and let Harmon's wagon pull abreast of him. Over the noise of the creaking, jolting freight wagon he pulled up to Harmon's mule. "What's ahead of us?" he asked.

Dave yanked down his neckerchief and said, *"Malpais.* A mile-long stretch of it."

Lieutenant Overman nodded his acknowledgment of this information and then moved on ahead, passed the supply wagon and the ambulance and went on toward Sergeant Noonan in the point position. When he reached Noonan, he reined in to match the pace of the sergeant's horse.

"That's *malpais,* isn't it, Sergeant?"

"Right, sir. Wicked, too, and hot."

Lieutenant Overman looked ahead, studying the

uneven skyline. He knew, but only by hearsay, that *malpais,* or bad rock, was of volcanic origin and was apt to be a jumbled mass of solidified lava that was all sizes and forms. He also knew that its razor-sharp edges could wear through a foot soldier's boots in a half-day's time. What he didn't know was how well a shod horse could handle the *malpais.*

"What's the road through it like, Noonan?" Overman asked.

"It's rough, sir, but not bad. Blow sand has kind of leveled it off." He shook his head. "I've heard the stage line spent plenty of powder to make it."

Lieutenant Overman persisted, "What's it like away from the road?"

Noonan looked at him and smiled. "Never heard of anyone trying it, sir."

Lieutenant Overman thought about this a moment, then said, "Looks like I pull my flankers in."

Noonan appeared to consider this, and then he shrugged. "It's your choice, Lieutenant. My guess is you'd be safe if you did. If a 'Pache put a barefoot pony into it off the road, he'd have to shoot 'im within the hour. His feet would be a bloody mush."

Overman nodded slowly. "What about men using the road to get into it, then forting up off the road?"

Noonan laughed. "An 'Pache moccasin hasn't been made that will go far in that rock. Besides, sir, 'Paches aren't much good fighting afoot. They like horses and a lot of space. They wouldn't have either of them in there."

"I'm not thinking about Apaches, Sergeant. The dead man wasn't an Apache that we found this morning."

Noonan said fervently, "Not by a long shot, he wasn't." He looked at Overman, his face showing concern. "Still, the only white men we've seen today were on the stage or on the stage escort." He hesitated. "Outside of Layton, his hostler, and that crazy prospector."

It was Overman's turn to concede, and he nodded agreement. "How do you figure that raid last night, Sergeant?"

Noonan shrugged again. "I think I know what they'd tell you at Whipple, Lieutenant. You see the placers at La Paz are mostly shut down. The boys working them are hanging around Ehrenburg without work or money to get out. At Whipple they figure the first day out of Ehrenburg or the last day into it is where trouble will happen. These miners gang up and will raid anything if they're strong enough. A day or so out of Ehrenburg and it's Indians you watch out for, not them."

"Why's that, Sergeant?"

"Simple, Lieutenant. The miners got no money for horse feed and no money for grub. They're too broke to stay out longer than overnight."

Lieutenant Overman turned this information over in his mind and it seemed to make sense. At this moment he wished fervently that Sergeant Noonan could be permanently under him. Here was a man who used his ears and eyes and who was full of information that he did not volunteer unless it was asked for. He was, Overman thought, the ideal type of non-commissioned officer—wise, willing, and seasoned.

By this time they were drawing near the *malpais,* and through the waves of heat that distorted everything in the distance Overman could see the jagged and wildly upended surfaces of the *malpais.* He said then, "Slack up a little, Sergeant, and wait for us at the *malpais.* I'll call the flankers in."

The lieutenant turned and rode back to the train, and Noonan felt a surge of quiet elation. He thought the lieutenant had believed him, and in fact everything Noonan had told him was true. The flankers, even on shod horses, would take an interminable time winding through that mass of *malpais.* Overman had no choice but to stick to the road.

If Kirby and his men had circled them during the day and were now forted up in the *malpais,* this would be easy. It would be simple enough to let the train get well into the *malpais,* shoot a lead horse on the first wagon and one on the rear wagon, thus blocking passage either way. Then it would be simple enough to pick off the detail from a higher vantage point. Once the escort was gone, Noonan didn't doubt that Harmon and his teamsters would surrender.

Dave Harmon had been regarding the *malpais*, too, and he was wondering how Lieutenant Overman would handle this. When he heard Overman's single rifle shot signaling in the flankers, a faint apprehension touched him. Overman was only doing what necessity dictated, but Dave knew that if the train was to be attacked, this would be the place for it. They would have no warning of the attack because the flankers were pulled in. They could not fort up or retreat because on that narrow road there was not room enough to turn the teams and wagons between the walls of the *malpais*.

He asked himself: Did he really think there was danger of attack? He simply didn't know. All day long he had watched the desert for signs of riders skirting them. He had seen nothing, but that didn't prove a thing.

They were close to the *malpais* when Overman signaled a halt. He rode back, passed Juliana and Thornton, and reined in beside Dave.

"I think we ought to take this as fast as your teams can make it, Harmon. You agree?"

"Expecting trouble?" Dave asked mildly. He was curious as to Overman's opinion of the situation.

"Not really," Overman said. Then he told Dave of Sergeant Noonan's modest judgment, which seemed to be the opinion of the Fort Whipple people who were used to escorting wagon trains and coaches—that danger of attack from all except Indians lay a day out of Ehrenburg.

When he had finished, Dave nodded, then said, "But there's always the exception, Dick."

Overman looked puzzled. "We've seen nothing today to cause alarm. I've questioned my flankers closely. They saw nothing."

Dave was silent, and his silence brought a faint expression of uneasiness to Overman's thin face. In self-justification, Overman said, "We've got to go through this if there're a hundred men in there; Dave. There's no way around it."

"True," Dave said quietly. "It all depends on *how* we go through it."

Overman frowned. "How we go through it? I don't see what you mean."

"Why, if the whole train is trapped in there, we're in for trouble." He paused to emphasize what came next "Why not send one wagon at a time through it? Under full escort, of course. If the first wagon gets through and the escort returns safely, then send the second. At some stage of the game they'll have to commit themselves, won't they?"

Overman thought about this. "What if half the wagons get through, then they attack the next one? Our party will be split."

"We still have the advantage," Dave said. "We'll have men on either side of them. Then we attack."

Slowly Overman's scowl of concentration erased itself. "Thunderation, you're right! That's the way we should do it. We'll have Miss Juliana and Thornton wait till the last, since we'll know by then if there's any danger." Overman sighed, and then gave a friendly grin. "I can see why you made a captaincy at your age, Dave."

Dave said nothing.

Overman sat lost in thought. When he spoke it was in a tone of command. "In case anything happens to me I want you to take command. Will you do that for me?"

"Of course," Dave said. "I'd just as soon my wagon didn't go first, though." At Overman's look of puzzlement, Dave said, "My wagon has most of the rifles. Let it be number three wagon. By that time we'll know where we stand."

"Good idea," Overman said. "Choose your wagon and teamster to send through first."

Dave tied his jerkline to his saddle horn, stepped out of the saddle, and went back to the wagon behind him and stopped beside the mounted teamster.

"Bailey, we're going through this *malpais* one at a time, under full escort. The lieutenant says I come last, so that's the way it's got to be. You'll go first, so pull out around me."

The teamster spoke laconically. "He expecting trouble?"

"No, he's just preparing for it." The driver nodded. Dave started the lead horse around the other wagon and watched it pass his own wagon, Thornton's supply wagon, and Juliana's ambulance, and then pull up for the escort to gather. He followed the wagon and halted beside Overman's horse. The trooper who had been driving Everts' wagon was again mounted on his own horse.

Overman said quietly to Dave, "If you hear any shooting, don't come after us. After all, if there is any fighting it'll be for the stuff in your wagons. If we're all trapped in there they'll get the wagons."

"All right," Dave said. He added quietly, "Luck to you," and turned and started back toward his wagon. As he passed the ambulance Juliana said, "What's going on, Dave?" He noted she had a veil over her face, as he had suggested. Now she unpinned it.

Thornton, who was standing in the blazing heat drinking from his canteen, saw Dave stop, and he came over in time to hear Dave say, "We're going through singly. The escort will take one wagon through, then come back for the next."

"Why, it'll take all night," Thornton said wearily. "What's behind this decision?"

"High rock overlooking a narrow road," Dave said mildly.

"What do you mean by that?" Juliana asked.

Patience was in Dave's tone of voice as he answered, "Why, if we're going to be attacked again like we were last night, this is the ideal place for the ambush."

A startled look came into Juliana's eyes. "You don't think—why, nobody's passed us today."

"Miss Juliana, all Dick is doing is playing it as safe as he can. Probably nothing will happen, but he owes it to all of us not to take a chance," Dave said.

"That's absolutely the most preposterous thing I ever heard," Thornton said.

"That's a fairly preposterous statement in itself," Dave said coldly.

"Is it?" Thornton said quickly. "Juliana has just

told you why it's preposterous. Isn't it true that nobody's passed us today? Have the flankers seen anything?"

Dave said mildly, "Thornton, you must come from a part of the country that's timbered."

"What's that got to do with it?" Thornton challenged.

"In timbered country anything moving sticks to the road. Here in the West we use the road only when it's the shortest distance between places."

"What is it you're trying to tell him?" Juliana asked.

"That anyone could have ridden around us and not have been seen," Dave said, still mildly.

Thornton snorted in disgust. "How will going singly help prevent trouble?"

When Dave told him, Thornton said promptly, "I'm willing to take Juliana's ambulance through this stretch and come back. If Overman will let me, I'll prove you've let your imagination get the better of your judgment."

"Go ask him," Dave said.

"I'll do that!" Thornton said sharply. He left them and went past Bailey's freight wagon and halted by Lieutenant Overman. Dave and Juliana watched their brief conversation.

"Doesn't John's suggestion make sense?" Juliana asked. "It would get us into King's Wells a lot sooner."

"If there are men in there, why would they shoot or even stop Thornton? Why would they show themselves to him?" He paused and added drily, "Thornton can't be sold. What's in the wagons can."

Now Thornton headed back toward them, and outrage was reflected in his stiff-legged walk. Coming up to the ambulance, he spoke to Juliana. "I was refused permission to try." There was derision in his voice, and now he looked at Dave. "I'm told you're in command while Lieutenant Overman and the detail are gone."

Dave nodded.

"Don't try and command me," Thornton warned. "You're a civilian and I'm a civilian. I'll do what I please."

Lieutenant Overman's order to mount broke off their conversation. The detail headed toward the break in the *malpais* and Bailey's teams got his wagon in motion. Two troopers dropped in behind him and in a matter of minutes they were out of sight at a bend of the road.

Kirby waited impatiently in the scalding heat of the *malpais*. It was too hot to sit down, and the heat from the rocks that came through the soles of his boots was almost unbearable. His lookout had told him half an hour ago that the train was nearing the *malpais*. But where was it? Earlier he and his men had passed down this road and had left their horses at King's Wells, which was on the eastern edge of the *malpais*. Now he had his men distributed on either side of the road, with orders to keep themselves hidden and to hold their fire until he shot first.

They had had a hard, hot ride from Layton's and they had not spared their horses. There would be plenty of fresh horses for them after this was over, he had told his men.

Brick had certainly picked an ideal spot, Kirby thought with grudging admiration. The whole train could be trapped here and easily overwhelmed, for his men had the enormous advantage of cover and height.

Now Kirby cocked his head and listened. In moments came the sound of many hoofbeats. Kirby smiled. He crouched lower and peered through the space between two irregular chunks of *malpais*. The train was approaching the spot directly below him. He could hear the heavy jolting of the wagon as it lumbered over the rock-floored road, and presently the officer commanding the detail came into sight. Behind him was a pair of troopers.

Another pair of troopers passed, then the teams, wagon, and the two troopers bringing up the rear. One of the latter was Brick Noonan, his sergeant's stripes plain.

Kirby waited for the second wagon, but it did not come. The racket made by the first wagon was slowly diminishing in volume, yet there was no sound of a following wagon. Kirby felt a swift uneasiness. What had happened? If the wagons were strung out far apart, then the first wagon would be past his last man before the last wagon was even with him.

He decided to risk a look, and he rose and peered over the rock at the stretch of road in the direction from which the wagon had come.

The road was empty.

Kirby had to come to an immediate decision. With unerring instinct he guessed the strategy they were using against possible attack—one wagon at a time. In those few moments he weighed the proper course of action. He did not know if the wagon passing contained the rifles; he did know that he could not afford to let it through. If he stopped it and the rifles weren't in it, then he could play his hole card; he could keep the whole train from water, without which they couldn't live. That being so, there was one other thing he had to do.

He swung his rifle up and took a careful sight on Brick Noonan's back. With eventual victory clearly in sight he did not intend to share the loot with Noonan. As he sighted, he thought, *You're a sucker, Brick;* then he squeezed the trigger. He could see Noonan driven over onto his horse's neck.

Lieutenant Overman scarcely had time to register the sound of the shot before all hell broke loose. He saw at one swift glance that they were shooting at his detail from both sides, front and rear. The lead horse of the freight team gave a shrill cry and went down, thrashing wildly and panicking the other teams. Overman knew instantly that the wagon was lost, and that if they stayed to fight this out the whole detail would be wiped out. Wheeling his horse and snapping a shot up the hill at a puff of smoke, Overman shouted, "Back! Back!"

Riding low over his horse's neck, he sped past the wagon. The other troopers, firing wildly at no visible target, preceded him. Lieutenant Overman skirted the downed horse and reined in beside the freight wagon. Bailey, the freighter, was marooned on his motionless mule. "Get behind me!" Overman said. A bullet whomped into the side of the wagon as the freighter scrambled out of the saddle and got up behind Overman.

Ahead of him Overman could see all his troopers save one were flattened in their saddles over the necks of their galloping horses; the one exception was Sergeant Noonan. His well-trained horse was standing, awaiting a command from the reins. Noonan was slumped over, his right hand clamping his left shoulder.

Overman seized the cheek strap of Noonan's horse, turned him, and then cut the horse viciously across the rump with his gauntlets. The horse lunged, and Noonan barely managed to stick to the saddle as the horse went into a gallop.

Now Overman spurred his own horse savagely and the bullets seemed to be hunting them out. Bailey, whose arms were around his waist, suddenly clamped him with a savage grip that almost cracked his ribs. Overman knew that Bailey was hit, and he prayed that the man could hold on until they were out of danger.

Bullets were ricocheting off rocks on either side of them and Overman felt a sudden hurtful slam in his thigh. In a moment then they were out of range and the firing died down.

Overman turned in the saddle and said over his shoulder, "Are you hurt?"

"Got a broke arm, I think."

Only then did Overman realize that it was Bailey's left arm that was clasping him. There was no pressure at all from the right arm. His own leg still stung from the ricochet.

Ahead of him his reined-in troopers were waiting.

When the fusillade began, the sound of it came plainly to the train. The teamsters were gathered in a group by themselves in the shade of the wagons. Dave and John Thornton were standing on either side of the ambulance that held Juliana.

It was Thornton who spoke first, and with excitement. "We'd better get in there and help them!"

"Overman said not to," Dave said mildly.

"Are you going to let them be butchered?" Thornton asked hotly.

Dave looked at him coldly across Juliana. "That's one of the things you sign up for when you join the Army." Dave turned and called to his men, "Get your rifles, boys." Then to Juliana he said, "If anybody but the military comes out of that cut, Miss Juliana, I want you to climb into the front corner of my wagon. There's a place made for you in the freight. Thornton, here's my pistol." He gave his hand gun to Thornton, who accepted it reluctantly.

By now the firing had ceased, and Dave waited impatiently. The sun was almost down and it cast long grotesque shadows ahead of them. He was thankful now that his wagon with the rifles had been held back. The kegs of nails, the barrels of flour, the horseshoes, and the bolts of calico that were in the first wagon wouldn't stack up to much loot for the attackers.

Now plainly visible in the low sun, the troopers came out of the cut. Dave counted them and saw one horse and rider being led and a pair riding double. As they approached Dave saw that it was Noonan's horse that was being led.

Turning to Juliana, he said, "We've got at least one hurt man, Miss Juliana." Then he went out to meet the troopers and Thornton followed him. Juliana turned in her seat to reach for her valise and the clothing in it that she would tear up for bandages.

Lieutenant Overman reined in. His slim face held a quiet rage as he said, "Better move your teamster over in the supply wagon, Dave. This man's hurt badly. Sergeant Noonan got it, too."

Without speaking, Dave went back to the supply wagon, followed by the detail and Juliana. Lieutenant Overman called over his shoulder, "Mister Thornton, please keep an eye on that road. If anybody comes out of it, warn us."

Once Everts was moved to one side, Bailey was laid out on the pallet. Noonan was helped down off his horse and was propped up against the wheel of the supply wagon. His blouse was stained with blood from a shoulder wound.

While Juliana and Dave splinted up Bailey's smashed arm with slats ripped off the cases of canned goods, Overman and one of the troopers attended Noonan's wound. The bullet had gone into Noonan's shoulder through the heavy muscle, had broken his collarbone, and lay just under the skin of his upper chest. He seemed to Overman to be in a state of shock. Overman first split the skin over the bullet with his knife, and removed the bullet. He washed the wound and bandaged it, and then made a sling for Noonan's left arm out of his trooper's neckerchief. Through all of it Noonan did not utter a sound of pain, nor did he talk. He accepted the canteen of water and drank from it, but it was as if the bullet had stricken him dumb.

Lieutenant Overman called over to the troopers who were describing the attack to the teamsters. "Cleary, relieve Mister Thornton. You'll act as sentry until relieved."

Overman caught Dave's eye and motioned toward the empty ambulance. When Dave left the supply wagon, Juliana followed him. Thornton, relieved by the trooper, headed for the ambulance, too, so that all four met there. Lieutenant Overman then told them briefly of the ambush.

"How many guns would you judge?" Dave asked.

"A dozen, Dave, maybe more, but I wasn't taking time to count them." He looked at them all now, and said, "You can see what our situation is. We're blocked from water. They have the commanding position and I don't think we can dig them out with twice the men we have available. Do you, Dave?"

"No," Dave said. He looked about him in the dusk. "I don't want to interrupt you, Dick, but we're wide open for a raid here. Can we get our wagons corralled and the stock inside before dark?"

"You're right," Overman said. "We'll talk afterwards."

By full dark the wagons were formed in a circle with the animals inside it. Sentries were out and two fires were going. Then Juliana, Dave, Overman, and Thornton, while the coffee came to a boil, drew together again. It was Thornton who came up to the fire last. In his once white shirt, his townsman's trousers and shoes, he looked grotesquely out of place, Dave thought.

And it was Thornton who spoke first. "Lieutenant, may I make a suggestion in all good faith?"

"Why, of course."

Thornton looked carefully at the three of them and then asked rhetorically, "What are these men after that attacked us?"

"Why, our rifles, of course," Overman said.

"Then why don't we give the rifles to them?" Before anyone could answer him, Thornton went on. If we give them the rifles they'll let us alone. They'll let us go through to water."

This was such an amazing and unlooked-for suggestion that all of them were silent. Thornton, seeing that he had them at a momentary advantage, pushed his case. He was excited now. His eyes were bright in the firelight, and when he talked he made short, chopping gestures with his soft hands.

"Lieutenant Overman, you were assigned this detail with the thought in mind that you would protect not only the lone woman, but the civilian men."

"And the freight," Dave cut in.

"Freight?" Thornton echoed. "Is any freight worth the lives of men and women?" He looked directly at Overman. "Surely you've read enough military history, Lieutenant, to know that commanders have abandoned supplies, weapons, ammunition, and even friends in order to save the lives of their men. Remember Bull Run? You think Pope didn't abandon equipment?"

"I don't think Colonel Bowie at the Alamo requested safe conduct," Overman countered drily. "He neither deserted his friends there nor abandoned his equipment." He added, "And, like us, he was outnumbered."

Thornton's faced paled with anger. "Whose decision was it, Lieutenant, to send that wagon in alone, with my supplies?"

"It was mine," Overman said.

Thornton countered swiftly. "What right have

you to sacrifice my supplies over army supplies? If
you thought something was going to be lost, why
shouldn't it be the rifles, and not my trade goods?"

Dave said drily, "Here's the man from timber
country talking again."

"Then you answer my question!" Thornton challenged Dave.

Dave said patiently, "One, those rifles are needed
at Fort Whipple. Two, if we surrender them we arm
that many Indians who'll use them to kill us with."

"We're close to being killed now!" Thornton said
hotly.

Lieutenant Overman spoke up then and there
was command in his voice. "You asked if you could
make a suggestion in good faith, Mister Thornton. You
have. Your suggestion is unacceptable."

"Then what do you plan to do? Let us die here?"
Thornton demanded.

For the first time that day Dave saw a glint of
humor creep into Overman's eyes.

"Since you asked to make a suggestion, Mister
Thornton, I think Dave should be allowed to make
a suggestion. He's responsible for the goods and the
rifles. And, like you, he also has his life at stake."
He looked at Dave. "Have you a suggestion, Dave?"

"Yes. Pull stakes at moonrise and go back to
Layton Wells."

Lieutenant Overman smiled. "That would be my
suggestion, too, Mister Thornton, and that's what
we'll do."

"You've got your heads together on this!" Thornton cried, his voice close to shrill. "You've decided it
without considering other opinions!"

"As it happens, we haven't got together," Overman said. "However, I'm as grateful to Dave for his
opinion as I am to you for yours."

Thornton looked at Juliana. "Juliana, does this
make any sense to you? If we'd only turn over the
rifles we could reach Fort Whipple and your family
without any more trouble."

There was a long moment of silence as Juliana
considered this. "I'm sure the Apaches would give

our people safe conduct only if we'd move out of the country," she said. Then she added, "I'm hungry. I don't know about the rest of you."

Thornton turned angrily and left the fire. Juliana knew she had wounded him deeply, and that he would probably sulk during the rest of the trip. It was strange how the events of the past few days had changed her liking for John Thornton into near dislike. He seemed to have a gifted tongue which seemed dedicated to saying the wrong thing at the wrong time.

Dave dished up two plates of food and went over to the supply wagon where Bailey and Everts were lying with a dim-lit lantern at their heads.

Juliana dished up plates for Lieutenant Overman and herself, and then took her seat again on an open crate of canned peaches.

"Everybody's made a suggestion but me, Dick. Am I permitted to make one? In good faith, too?"

Lieutenant Overman smiled. "Go ahead, it's your turn."

"I would like to suggest that everyone here is grateful to you for handling these killers the way you did. If we'd gone in there blindly. I think we'd all be dead."

Lieutenant Overman flushed with embarrassment, then he said, "I'd like to claim credit for the plan, but it was Dave's idea."

"Then I'm grateful to him, too."

Overman nodded solemnly. "So am I."

Juliana began to eat, but Overman had stopped eating and was staring at the fire. "I can't help but wonder why he left the Army."

"He told me he was invalided out because of his eye."

Overman shook his head. "If he said that it must be true. Still, I've met a dozen officers who aren't perfect physical specimens. My commanding officer at Fort Mohave lost an arm at Bull Run. I used to know a major at Camp McDowell who was so crippled with rheumatism he had to be lifted on and off a horse."

Juliana said nothing, and Overman continued.

"Maybe that missing eye is the handiest excuse to cover the real reason."

Juliana looked up. "You're not implying that he was discharged for something he had done?"

Overman looked surprised. "I would never imply that, Miss Juliana—not after today. No, what I meant was that poor pay or family troubles or a business opportunity might have influenced him. I think—"

He saw Dave approaching at the very edge of the firelight, and he stopped speaking and turned his attention to the food on his plate. Dave came over, dished out his food, sat down, and began to eat.

"Remember when moonrise is, Dave?" Overman asked.

"Around eleven."

"How's your water situation? I noticed the hostler filling barrels back at Layton's."

"We're all right," Dave said. "Traveling at night will help too."

Lieutenant Overman finished eating and rose, saying, "I'd better go tell the men our plans so they can get some rest."

"If you want to double your guard, call on my men," Dave said. "On me too."

Overman nodded and moved over to the other campfire. Dave saw that Sergeant Noonan was eating with the rest of the troopers.

As Dave began to eat he saw Juliana, who had finished, staring into the meager flames. He could guess her thoughts. She was wondering how this would end, and Dave had to confess that he was a little puzzled himself. They could reach Layton Wells on the water that was in the barrels ironed to the side of his wagons, but beyond that he didn't know. The eastbound stage, not due for a week, would undoubtedly be passed through the *malpais*. The question that bothered him more than anything else, however, was what their attackers would do when they discovered that the train was headed back for Layton Wells. If they decided to attack the train, either at night or in the daytime, the train would be halted and forced to corral. Then again they would be at the mercy of this gang that barred them from water.

Suddenly Juliana's voice interrupted his thoughts. "Dick gives you credit for saving the train today."

Dave looked up with a smile. "Who did the fighting?"

"But who had the idea? If we'd all gone in there together I don't think we'd have come out," Juliana said.

"I knew the country and Dick didn't. It's as simple as that."

"I think he's a good officer, don't you?"

Dave nodded. "He's good now, and he'll be better."

Juliana looked at him, hesitated, then said abruptly, "We were discussing your career, Dick and I."

Dave frowned, and the movement of his forehead pushed his eyepatch down a little. He touched it back into place before he said, "Neither of you knows anything about it, do you?"

Juliana went on with seeming irrelevance, "Dick's commanding officer at Fort Mohave lost an arm at Bull Run. A senior officer at Camp McDowell is so crippled with rheumatism he has to be helped on a horse. Then why were you invalided out?"

Dave watched her a long moment before he answered. "I'm not trying to be impertinent, but why do you care?"

"Because I think you belong in the Army. Nobody has to tell me or Dick that you were a good officer. You showed it today without ever leading a man."

Dave put down his plate and then spoke slowly. "One way or another, I guess we're all victims of circumstance. You became one when you joined this train. I became one when I was transferred to a weak command."

Juliana looked puzzled.

Dave continued, "I came in from the field to serve under a man who had a soft job that he was afraid he'd lose if my major was promoted. He would go to any length to discredit the major. His way of doing it was through me. He complained of my work and doubted my physical ability to continue serving

in the Army. This let him discredit my major's judgment before review boards. He consistently questioned
my major's judgment in overlooking my infirmity."
Dave added wryly, "In other words, he was using me
to stop the promotion of my major."

"Couldn't you request a transfer?" Juliana asked.

"It was turned down," Dave said. "I was too use-
ful to him as a whipping boy."

"So you resigned?"

"Because my career was stopped. I couldn't hope
for a promotion, and neither could my major."

Juliana said musingly, "There are people in the
Army like that, Dad says."

Dave nodded. "There are people like that anywhere, and they mostly get found out, just like my
colonel did."

"Found out?"

Dave nodded. "The year after I resigned my commission, the good colonel was convicted of channeling
anything salable to the merchants of the garrison town
and pocketing the money."

"But it was too late to help you."

Dave nodded, then smiled reminiscently, "But
not too late to help my major. He's now a brigadier
general, and there'll never be a better one."

Lieutenant Overman came up to the fire then
and said, "I just sent my boys to bed. I think I'd better
send you two."

"I think you'd better, too," Dave said.

Before he rolled into his blankets, Dave checked
his two teamsters in the supply wagon. Everts was
asleep, but Bailey was awake and feverish. There was
pain in his eyes, but both men knew there was nothing
to be done about it.

Afterwards, so as to be near Bailey and Everts,
Dave threw his blankets under the supply wagon and
rolled in. In the few minutes before sleep came to him,
he wondered why he had talked so openly to Juliana
about his past. Had it seemed to her that he was an
embittered crybaby? He didn't think so, or at least
he had not intended it to sound that way. Outside of
the few transient officers he had served with, he had

never told this bit of his history. It was important only to himself and was past.

Maybe because Juliana was part of the Army, and because her father would undoubtedly tell her the story, it didn't seem to him that he had been seeking sympathy. He had tried to make a simple statement of fact and it seemed to him that she accepted it as such. She was, Dave thought, a tough and perceptive girl, frank to bluntness, and he admired her because this was so.

6

Sergeant Brick Noonan lay in his blankets and listened to the activity and talk of the camp slowly die down. His shoulder throbbed with every beat of his pulse. Once again he reviewed the events of the afternoon that led to his intentional wounding. He had told Kirby at the very beginning to warn the men against shooting at a uniform that bore sergeant's stripes since he himself would be wearing that uniform. The shot that hit him came from the left, on which arm he wore his sergeant's chevrons. There could be no mistake about it; the shot was deliberate.

According to his own close reasoning, Noonan was certain that Kirby had fired the shot. Noonan thought he knew why. Kirby was the only man in this collection of riffraff who would have the brains to assess the situation there in the *malpais*. Kirby undoubtedly saw that he was in complete command of the situation, that he could successfully bar the wagon train from water, and that the guns would eventually be his, either by waiting for the train to run out of water and surrender, or by attacking it when it moved and forcing it to corral, still without water. That being the case, why should he, Kirby, share with another man the loot from the sale of the guns?

So Kirby had shot him, just as he would have shot Kirby in similar circumstances. *Only I'd have made sure I killed him,* Noonan thought. That's where Kirby had made his mistake. Troopers of the detail had told Noonan that for moments, when his horse had halted and he was in a state of shock, he was a sitting duck for a good many of the rifles. Apparently Kirby thought he had done the job; the others had been warned not to shoot at him.

When Kirby learned that his bullet in the back had been too high, then Noonan · knew that Kirby would not stop until he had succeeded in killing him. From now on Noonan was number one on Kirby's list.

Ever since the pain of his wound had slacked off a little, Noonan knew what he was going to do. Now he listened to the small night noises of the sleeping camp— The stirring of horses within the circled wagons, the snoring of the exhausted men and, even more faintly, the slow pacing of the sentries. He waited another fifteen minutes to be sure the camp was asleep, and then painfully crept out of his blankets. He made sure that his pistol was in its holster before stooping down to pick up his hat. As he strolled out away from the wagons, he put on his hat, and waited until one of the sentries on his round approached.

"Cleary," he called softly.

"Who is it?" a voice challenged.

"Me. Noonan." Noonan walked up to the sentry, who halted.

"I'm going for a walk. Don't shoot me."

"What the hell for?" Cleary demanded.

"I can't sleep with this shoulder," Noonan said. "If I walk around the wagons I'll spook somebody and they'll take a shot at me."

Cleary was silent a moment. There was sense in what Noonan said, but he knew what would happen if Overman spotted Noonan's absence. But why should he? He wasn't counting his men on the hour. Besides, what harm would it do to let Noonan past?

"Go ahead," Cleary said. "Only remember, we're breaking camp when the moon rises."

"'I'll be back long before that," Noonan said. He moved past Cleary and within seconds was lost in the darkness.

Noonan made his exit from the camp and headed west. Now he made a wide circle of the camp, picked up the road, and headed east toward the near *malpais*. He wondered, grimly, if Kirby's guard would shoot first or challenge him. He wasn't long in finding out.

He had moved into the *malpais* less than a quarter-mile when a gun flared in the road ahead of him. The bullet ricocheted off the road and whistled as it touched his hat.

"Quit it!" Noonan shouted. "It's me! Noonan! Brick Noonan!"

"Put a light on yourself," a voice called back.

Brick was ready for this too. He pulled out a match from his blouse pocket, wiped it alight, and held it in front of his face. He heard the sound of approaching boots and he waited. Undoubtedly the shot could have been heard at the wagon train, but what did it matter? He was more concerned as to whether it had been heard in Kirby's camp.

A man approached, and Noonan said, "Who is it?"

"Bill Earl."

"Where you camped?"

"At the Wells." There was a pause. "They know, back there you're gone?"

"I just walked out," Noonan said. "I'm with Kirby from now on." Then he added, "Move up closer to the edge of the *malpais*. They'll be breaking camp at moonrise. Keep an eye on them."

At the man's grunt of assent, Noonan went on. Presently he came to the captured wagon, and out of curiosity he struck another match against the wagon side to see what Kirby had done with the freight. It had simply been dumped into the *malpais*, undoubtedly the result of Kirby's hopeful search for the rifles. Ahead of the wagon two dead horses had been dragged to the side of the road. Their legs were stiff, their bellies bloated. The other three teams, Noonan knew, were probably at Kirby's camp.

He walked on, and began to feel a lassitude that he knew he must fight. He had lost a lot of blood before his shoulder had been attended to, and it was telling on him. Ahead of him he could dimly see a notch in the night sky that told him he was approaching the end of the *malpais*. And now he lifted his gun from its holster. As quietly as possible he moved forward, wondering if Kirby would have a sentry posted at the camp.

He saw the man before the sentry saw or heard him. The man was outlined against the night sky as he slowly tramped back and forth across the road. Noonan moved silently toward him until he was within earshot and then said quietly, "It's me, Brick Noonan."

The sentry wheeled and lifted his rifle.

"Don't shoot. I'll strike a match," Brick said evenly. Again he struck a match and held it in front of his face, and the sentry came forward.

"Was that you that shot?" the sentry said.

"That was Bill Earl shooting at me," Noonan said. "Did it wake the camp?"

"No. It was too far off The man paused. "Are you hurt?"

Noonan threw the match away. "A little," he said. "Know where Kirby's sleeping?"

"I'll show you."

"Let's go quiet," Noonan said. "No sense in waking everybody."

The man moved ahead and Noonan followed. Only a few yards beyond where the *malpais* ended was the old adobe stage station that had been abandoned. As at all desert wells, there were stunted trees around the water. Noonan could see well enough now to note that the men were scattered over the bare ground between the spring and the adobe. The guard circled them, and finally halted near a snoring figure.

Brick whispered now, "Let me wake him. Got a candle?"

For answer the man moved over to the edge of the spring, leaned down, and picked up a lantern, which he handed to Noonan. "Kirby got it from Layton today."

"Good. You better get back to your post." The sentry turned and disappeared into the night. Now Brick gently put the bale of the lantern in his left hand and found he couldn't hold it, so he pushed the bale up around his wrist. Softly, gently, he cocked the gun, muzzling its click against his blouse before he walked silently to where Kirby lay sleeping. Kirby was on his back and Noonan could hear his even breathing.

Then Noonan pointed his gun and shot Kirby in the face.

The bellow of the gun brought the men out of their blankets, and Noonan called out again, "It's me, Brick Noonan. Don't shoot."

"What was that shot?" somebody called.

"Come over and see, all of you," Brick said, and the men stumbled toward him in the darkness. To the first man who approached, Brick handed the lantern. "Light it," he commanded.

The man set the lantern on the ground beside Kirby, lifted the chimney, struck a match, and lit the wick. Only then by its light did he see Kirby. He dropped the match and jumped back, and then looked at Noonan.

"Take a look, all of you," Noonan said in a voice of iron.

The men did. One brief glance was enough for most of them; afterwards they looked at Noonan.

"Why'd you do that?" one of them asked.

Noonan touched his bandaged shoulder. "Because he shot me in the back today." Noonan looked around the group, and he was smiling faintly. "Anybody object?"

None of them spoke up to ask how Noonan could be sure that it was Kirby who shot him. Kirby, never their real boss, was dead. Noonan, always their real boss, was still in command.

"A couple of you lug him into that adobe there, then come back." Two men stepped forward, picked up Kirby's slack form, and put him just inside the door of the tumbled-down building. The other men watched them go and return.

"Now listen, all of you," Brick said. "The wagon

train is heading back to Layton's at moonrise. Once they're strung out, we'll attack them. They'll have to corral again, and that's just the way I want them. We'll hold them there until their water gives out."

He paused. "Better saddle up now. Let your horses drink, but fill your canteens first."

As the men squatted to pick up their canteens, Brick looked at the adobe. By the dim light of the lantern he could see Kirby's boots. He thought: *It was your own idea, Kirby. How do you like it now?*

Private Cleary halted in alarm at the distant sound of the shot which came from the *malpais*. Should he wake Lieutenant Overman to tell him? If he did, he ran the risk that Overman would rouse the camp and discover that Sergeant Noonan was missing. Had Noonan fired the shot, he wondered. No, Noonan had headed in the other direction.

For an agonized moment of indecision, Cleary knew what he had to do. Since the other three sentries were freighters, it was his duty as a trooper to inform his lieutenant of the shot. He went over to the freight wagon under which Overman was sleeping and found the lieutenant standing beside the wagon.

"You heard the shot, sir?"

"I heard it," Overman said slowly. "I wonder what it means?"

"I couldn't guess, sir. Quite a ways off, though."

"Right. Go back to your post, Cleary. Report anything you see or hear."

"Yes, sir." Cleary walked away from the wagon with a vast sense of relief. Overman was not going to alert the camp after all. Now all Cleary had to worry about was Noonan being discovered by the lieutenant when he came back to camp. Well, that really wasn't his worry. When it came down to it, he had simply deferred to a sergeant who outranked him.

Cleary's stretch of ground to guard paralleled the road, and when he reached its easternmost limit he met one of the teamster's sentries.

"Who's shooting?" the sentry said.

"Don't know. But the lieutenant heard it. If you hear anything, walk back and tell him."

"If I hear anything, I'll run back," the teamster said drily.

Cleary turned and slowly walked his beat. When he came to the western end of it he paused. He was about to turn when he caught the ever-so-faint sound of footsteps out in the darkness.

He listened as they came closer. Then he called out softly, "Noonan, get back in your blankets."

The footsteps halted, and then a strangely hoarse voice said, "I'm not Noonan. I'm Trooper Adams."

Instantly Cleary brought up his rifle and said harshly, "Stand where you are, trooper!"

Slowly, his rifle ready, Trooper Cleary advanced. When he was close enough to see the almost diminutive figure of Trooper Adams, he halted. "Identify yourself," he said.

"John Francis Adams, Squadron F, Fifth Regiment on special detail out of Camp McDowell." His voice was still hoarse, and now he cleared his throat.

"What the hell are you doing out here?" Cleary demanded.

"You army?" Adams asked.

Cleary now realized that his challenge was unorthodox and that this man had no way of identifying him as belonging to the Army. "I'm Trooper Jim Cleary, out of Fort Mohave," he said.

"Where's you commanding officer?" Adams asked.

"You got a match?"

"No, have you?"

"No," Cleary answered. "I'm going to put my rifle in your back. Don't try to run or I'll let it off."

"Run," Trooper Adams said with quiet derision. "You couldn't make me run."

Trooper Cleary circled him, then prod... with his rifle barrel. "Straight ahead and ... left. You'll see the wagons in a minute..."

It was less than a minute. Th... by the wagon under which Li... his blankets. Cleary said ... awake, sir?"

"Yes, Cleary," Overman said sleepily.

"I've got a man here says he's army. Can you strike a light, sir?"

Overman tumbled out of his blankets, fumbled in his pockets for a match, and struck a light. Before him he saw a small man, not much more than a boy. His blouse held the salt rime of sweat and his boots were in tatters. His face, oddly white, held a blond fuzz of beard, and the whites of his eyes, under swollen lids, were deeply blood-shot. He seemed to Overman on the verge of exhaustion.

The match went out and Overman said, "Sit down, trooper. Cleary, get him some food." Overman turned to the lantern hanging on the side of the wagon, struck another match, and lighted the lantern. He set it on the ground beside Trooper Adams, who had accepted Lieutenant Overman's invitation to sit down.

Out of the darkness Dave Harmon materialized as Overman extended a canteen to Adams. Hearing him approach, Overman turned to regard Dave, who gave him a quizzical look, but said nothing.

Adams drank until Overman reached down, pulled the canteen away from his mouth, and said, "Easy does it."

When Adams relinquished the canteen, Overman said quietly, "Now, who are you?"

Trooper Adams identified himself, then briefly told his story of Lieutenant Miller's detail. When he mentioned that the detail consisted of nine men and an officer, Overman glanced quickly at Harmon. In a tone-

Adams told of killing Reardon, finishing with, "or him, sir. I don't reckon I could have stacked up to here if he'd hit me."

"you walked?" Overman asked.

At that was slow going."

"d you find the spot where

"I followed a true this road, I

food and

a cup of cold coffee. Adams took them and began to wolf the food down, eating like an animal.

Both Lieutenant Overman and Dave watched him in silence, not speaking until his plate and cup were emptied. Then Overman asked, "How far do you reckon your detail is from here?"

"Forty miles maybe, Lieutenant. I can't rightly tell. I had to rest a lot on account of the heat."

"You say they had rations for another week?"

"Rations for ten men, sir."

Overman looked at Dave and tilted his head. Both men walked out of earshot of Adams. Now three of the troopers, roused by the talk, came up to the lantern and began to quiz Adams, who answered their questions in a toneless voice of exhaustion.

Overman halted ahead and waited for Dave to come up to him. Then Overman remarked wryly, "Trouble on trouble, eh?"

"Good luck on bad luck, Dick," Dave answered.

Overman regarded him with mild surprise. "How do we fight off this gang and still help Miller's stranded detail?"

Dave said thoughtfully, "Why not let me take ten horses and ride down to them?"

"With ten horses missing, you think we can make it to Layton's?" Overman asked dubiously.

"Let's forget Layton's," Dave said.

"You mean stay here?"

Dave said, "With ten horses gone our water will go further, won't it?"

"True," Overman said. "But we'll have to move sometime."

"But when we move we'll have Miller's men added to your escort. With that many extra man we might fight our way through to King's Wells. Maybe we won't have to go back to Layton's."

Overman was silent for so long that Dave shifted his feet in impatience. Presently Overman said, "It just might work. I reckon they won't attack us here while you're gone, and if they did I think we could drive them off. Why should they attack when they figure we're out of water and they're keeping us from reaching it?"

Dave nodded assent. The whole camp was awake by now and most of the men were clustered around Trooper Adams, listening again to the story of his incredible journey. Juliana, and even Thornton, came over to question Overman about what was happening.

It was then that Overman announced the change in plans. Dave and one of his teamsters were to leave at moonrise with horses for the stranded troopers. The rest of the detail was to stay forted up here, and in the unlikely event they were attacked they had enough guns to defend themselves.

Lieutenant Overman then went over to the group clustered around Adams and described the new plan. When he was finished, he looked around the men. "Where's Sergeant Noonan?" he asked.

"I'll get him," one of the troopers said. He disappeared into the darkness and presently returned. "He's not in his blanket, sir," the trooper reported.

"All right, Mahoney, go out and relieve the sentries, one by one. Tell them to report to me. Don't leave until you're relieved."

To the still seated Adams he said, "Trooper Adams, roll into my blankets there. Get some sleep. Bosworth, you and Keef get a lantern and cut out the dozen best mounts we've got. No mules."

The men scattered and Lieutenant Overman came back to Dave, who was stuffing food for himself and his teamster in the saddle bags with Juliana's help. Thornton was watching them, and Overman came up in time to hear Thornton ask sullenly, "How many days will this add?"

"I can answer that, Mister Thornton," Overman said flatly. "It'll take as many days as necessary."

Now one of Dave's teamsters who had been on sentry duty approached. "You wanted me?"

"Yes. Did you pass Sergeant Noonan through the lines? Did you hear or see him pass through?"

"Not me."

"Then get back to your post."

Private Cleary was the second sentry, and Overman put the same question to him.

"Yes, sir, I passed him," Cleary said. "His shoulder was hurting him so that he couldn't sleep. He said he wanted to walk but that he was afraid someone might shoot him if he kept close to the wagons."

Dave looked at Overman and said, "That could explain the shot we heard."

"Did he seem delirious to you, Cleary?"

"I couldn't see him, sir, but he sounded like he was hurting."

Overman scowled. "We'll have to wait till morning before we look for him. I can't risk my detail hunting down a stray trooper who isn't even attached to it."

Juliana asked slowly, "You think he might have deserted to those people?"

"Hardly," Overman said. "They shot him today, didn't they?"

Although Dave held his silence, he thought Juliana could be right. He remembered the excellent horse Noonan rode and Noonan's story of how he acquired it. He also remembered Noonan's lack of papers, which Overman had sensibly ignored out of gratitude for an added rifle.

If Noonan had deserted to the enemy, there was little he could tell them that they didn't already know. One thing Noonan couldn't tell them was Overman's decision to stay here and wait for the stranded detail.

Just after moonrise the supply wagon was pushed out of the circle, and Dave, mounted on Noonan's horse, rode through the break. He was followed by ten more animals with his teamster Solly Liston bringing up the rear. They headed west, picking up the road they had traveled over earlier that day. Three miles from camp Dave spotted the cairn Trooper Adams had built to mark the trail he had made through the desert. Dave, in the lead, and the band of horses turned south.

The *malpais* still held the heat of the day, but it was bearable. The jagged upended mass of rock took on weird and monstrous shapes in the moonlight, and Noonan's men, waiting in the road, studied them curiously, commenting on their fantastic forms.

Noonan himself was a hundred yards away at the west entrance to the *malpais,* Bill Earl beside him. They had seen the lanterns lighted up and had assumed that the train was making up for travel. Dave's exit with the horses had gone unnoticed by them, since the wagons lay between Noonan and Dave.

Now the lanterns were being doused and Bill Earl looked quizzically at Noonan. "It don't look like they aim to move tonight."

"They'll move," Noonan said flatly. "I heard the lieutenant give the orders."

They waited impatiently for another half-hour, but all lanterns were out. The camp looked asleep except, of course, for the sentries Noonan knew were out. His wound was nagging now, and he felt a growing anger. At first he had thought the lanterns indicated that the train was getting ready to move; now he wondered if his absence had been discovered and if the lanterns had been lighted to search for him.

But why wasn't the train being readied to move? Had his desertion alarmed Overman to the extent that he had changed plans? Why should it alarm him? If Overman questioned Cleary, all the trooper could tell him was that Sergeant Noonan had taken a walk out into the night.

Bill Earl's voice interrupted his thoughts. "Hell, the camp's asleep," he said in disgust. "They're waiting for daylight."

"Maybe they are," Brick agreed reluctantly. He had the strongest of impulses to attack the camp right now, but he also had an old soldier's appreciation of the situation. The camp could be easily defended against five times the number of his men. Now that the moon was up, surprise was out of the question. They had the protection of the wagons, while his own men would be exposed on the flat moonlit desert. No, it would be foolhardy to risk an attack and lose advantage of numbers.

Now Brick said with assumed cheerfulness, "Looks like we don't have to worry about them moving."

"I thought you wanted 'em to move?" Bill said.

Brick shook his head. "Why would I want 'em to move? If they started to move and we attacked, they'd fort up again. They might just as well be here as a mile down the road. Wherever they are, they'll be using up water."

He turned and swung up on his horse. "Stay here until I send someone to relieve you, Bill."

"You going back to camp?"

"That's it. I'd rather sleep than watch them sleep."

John Thornton came awake at earliest light and lay in his blankets thinking of the events of last night. It seemed to him that this whole business was the sheerest idiocy. Why should they be suffering these hardships for the sake of a few rifles that the Army could easily replace? Undoubtedly the Army wasn't in need of the rifles or they would have sent many more men and used a far speedier method of transporting them than these lumbering freight wagons.

He thought now of Sergeant Noonan's disappearance. Had the man deserted, as Juliana suspected, or had he walked off in delirium into the desert? Maybe he, too, was sick of being tied down to danger and privation by the presence of five crates of rifles.

Come to think of it, why couldn't he leave, too?

The thought brought a strange surge of excitement. What was there to stop him from walking into the camp of their attackers? They didn't want him; they wanted the rifles. In fact, they would probably welcome him, since it would mean one less defender of the wagon train. Then, too, he should have no trouble getting a mount. After all, the attackers had extra horses from the lost freight wagon. He could buy one of these horses and some food from them. Water was no problem, since there was a well ahead.

He pondered what Overman might say when he told him he was leaving. It didn't really matter what he said, because he had no authority over civilians. If Thornton chose to travel by himself, it was assuredly none of Overman's business. Anyway, why tell Overman anything? He was accountable to no one but himself.

What would Juliana think if he took off by himself? (Even in his own mind Thornton did not use the word desertion.) For some reason Juliana, these last few days, had grown away from him. Their friendship, which had ripened on shipboard, had been a precious thing to him at one time. He had even thought—no, intended—to ask her to marry him. Now he was glad he hadn't. A certain willfulness flawed her character. She had sided with Harmon against him too many times on this trip. While she was pretty, she seemed as strong-willed as any man, and he could not imagine being married to a woman who did not respect his judgment and his actions. No, Juliana was not for him. Therefore, why should she even enter into his consideration of going off alone?

The camp began to stir and Thornton rolled out of his blankets and put on his townsman's shoes. He was on his way to the nearest water barrel when he remembered Overman had forbidden them to wash with the precious water. It was at this moment that John Thornton, a man with almost a mania for cleanliness, made up his mind to desert.

At breakfast he found that, having missed supper last night, he was ferociously hungry. He saw Juliana and Overman at the small fire, went up to them, and gave them a good-morning. Juliana was mixing a batter of pan bread; one loaf was already baked and lay on a crate beside the fire. Overman was feeding more wood onto the fire.

Thornton went over to the round disc of bread, picked it up, and broke it in half.

"I was saving that for the hurt men, John," Juliana said.

"Oh, I didn't know," Thornton said coldly. He felt himself grow red.

"I'll take their breakfast to them as soon as I mix this."

Lieutenant Overman said, "I'll finish that, Miss Juliana, you go ahead with their breakfast."

As Juliana spooned out the stewed apples, which had been soaked overnight, and the bacon onto two plates, she ignored Thornton. Overman was busy with the batter.

When Juliana was out of earshot Thornton said, "You've had time to consider my suggestion about the rifles, Lieutenant. Are you of the same opinion to-day?"

Overman looked up and nodded. "And I will be tomorrow and the day after, Mister Thornton."

"I wonder what your superiors will say when I tell them of your decision?"

Lieutenant Overman stopped his stirring and stared at Thornton, his eyes hard. "They'll hear of it from me, not from you. And whatever they think, I'll take the consequences."

"I hope there are some."

"Just don't try to create any, Mister Thornton, or you're apt to be barred from Fort Whipple."

"I don't think you have that authority, Lieutenant."

"I don't claim it. I only claim that the Army punishes or rewards its own without outside help."

"We'll see," Thornton said.

Lieutenant Overman put the pan bread in the Dutch oven and then covered the oven with coals. Presently Juliana returned and reported that both Bailey and Everts seemed to be doing well and that Bailey's fever was almost gone.

"Aren't we torturing them unnecessarily?" Thornton asked her.

"What do you mean by that, John?"

"They both need medical attention. Why can't someone drive on ahead with them?"

Juliana looked at Lieutenant Overman, who was staring at Thornton. The lieutenant said drily, "Yourself, you mean?"

"I'd be willing to," Thornton answered calmly. "I'm not a soldier and I'm not a teamster. You could spare me."

"I could, but I won't," the lieutenant said grimly. "For your information, Thornton, both Everts and Bailey will be handling a rifle if we're attacked. So will Juliana. So will you." His voice held such contempt that Juliana looked away from Thornton.

When their breakfast was ready, it was full daylight and the blasting sun rose over the *malpais*. Again

there was not a cloud in the sky and the day appeared
to be like all the others since they had set out—mur-
derously hot and bright.

The conversation at breakfast was sparse and
strained, and Thornton knew that it was probably his
fault. However, he cared the least of the three.

Finished with breakfast, Thornton prowled the
camp. Troopers and teamsters were feeding and watering the horses and mules. On his round Thornton noted
that the lone daytime sentry had been pulled in to sit
in the shade of the wagons, since there was a clear
view of the road leading into the *malpais*.

Thornton returned to his gear under a wagon, got
his full canteen, slung it over his shoulder and moved
between the wagons. To the teamster sentry he said,
"I'm going to have a look at that black rock."

"I wouldn't if I was you," the teamster said un-
certainly.

"But you're not me," Thornton said. "I'm not
army, and I'm not working for Harmon. I'll do what I
please."

"Then if I was you, I'd stay wide of that road.
They'll have a man there sure."

"I intend to," Thornton said, and went on.

It was that easy. The troopers and teamsters were
occupied, and so were Overman and Juliana. If the
sentry had been a trooper, he would have informed
Overman immediately. But to a teamster, wholly without authority, Thornton's words made sense of a sort.
Nobody had authority over their civilian passengers.

Thornton headed for a part of the *malpais* well
away from the road. He was not challenged or called
back. When he reached the edge of the *malpais* he
turned and headed for the road. He was so far from
camp now that even if the sentry became alarmed there
was nothing to be done. He would be in the *malpais*
before they could reach him. Picking up the road now,
he turned into the *malpais*, already feeling the heat of
the road through his boots. He was less than fifty yards
into the rock before a man stepped out from behind a
huge chunk of lava, his rifle held at ready. The sentry

peered behind Thornton and cautiously came toward him.

"You from the train?"

"I am."

"We're awake. Go back and tell your soldiers to come through if they can."

"My good man, I'm leaving the train."

The man looked puzzled. "Footin' it?"

"You have extra horses. I want to buy one. Whom do I see?"

The sentry looked at him in bafflement. The situation was new to him. He'd been told to signal if the train started to move. Nobody had told him what to do if a fancy-talking man in a business suit and panama hat, a canteen slung over his shoulder, strolled into the *malpais* and asked to buy a horse. Perhaps this was some kind of a trap, he concluded. Slowly he walked up to Thornton and said, "Give me your gun."

"I don't have one."

The sentry laid his rifle aside, pulled a pistol, stepped up to Thornton and searched him, then stepped back. He looked more baffled than before. "Well, if you ain't got a gun, I don't reckon you can shoot me. Go on through, but you'll be on your own. I can't leave here."

"Thank you," Thornton said civilly. He tramped on.

The sentry stood in the road and watched him go, wondering what Noonan would do to him for letting him through.

Thornton walked on past the looted wagon and alarmed half a dozen vultures that were feasting on the carcasses of the horses. As he drew his handkerchief against the stench, the birds vaulted into the air on slowly flapping wings, then hovered overhead. When Thornton was well past the horses, he turned and saw the scavengers descending again.

At the edge of the *malpais* he was challenged by a second sentry who simply put a rifle in his belly and circled him, then put it in his back and prodded him into the camp close by.

Thornton counted eleven men lounging in the sparse shade of the trees around the spring. He also noticed the abandoned stage station. Part of the wall by the door had fallen into the interior, but Thornton had no way of knowing that this had been done only that morning. The adobe's wall had been caved in to cover Kirby's body.

As Thornton approached the men, none of them stood up, and Thornton recognized Sergeant Noonan seated among them.

"Ah, Sergeant. We seem to have had the same idea," Thornton said.

Noonan's face still held the shadow of pain but he managed a wry smile. "I know why I left. Why did you, Thornton?"

"Simply to get out of there."

Noonan scowled. "You got a message for me from Harmon or the lieutenant? They ready to quit?"

"No message," Thornton said. "I came on my own."

"To do what?" Brick asked, in a voice of puzzlement.

"Why, to travel on," Thornton said. "I'm not connected with Harmon or the Army. I see no reason for being punished for their bullheadedness."

"You don't?" Brick asked softly. "Just what do you plan to do?"

"I know you have extra horses from that freight wagon back there. Whom do I see about buying one?"

"You see me about it."

"Are all these men yours?" Thornton gestured to the listening men, none of whom had stirred from the shade.

"They're mine."

"Then you're not a soldier after all?"

"Only lately," Brick said drily.

"Ah," Thornton said. "Now I begin to understand. You're after the rifles, aren't you?"

"I am."

"You were to be the Trojan horse—the man in the enemy's camp."

"That's it," Brick admitted.

"Very clever," Thornton said. "Now, will you sell me a horse?"

"We'll talk about that later," Brick said. "Why didn't the train head back for Layton's place last night, like the lieutenant said?"

Thornton looked puzzled and then comprehension came. "Oh, you left before the strange trooper came in."

"Trooper?"

Thornton explained about Trooper Adams' appearance. He told of Dave's sudden decision to drive the mounts down to rescue Lieutenant Miller's detail. "With nine more men," Thornton said, "Overman thought they could battle their way through the *malpais*."

Noonan listened with sharp attention, then considered the news. He did not consult with any of his men, who were watching him with interest.

"Is that trooper sure those nine men are alive?"

"They were when he left."

Noonan reached up to his shoulder and absently felt of his bandaged wound. He was silent for so long that Thornton, standing in the sun, shifted impatiently. "May I sit in the shade?" he asked. Noonan didn't appear to hear him, and Thornton moved over and sat down by himself in a patch of shade.

Presently Noonan said, to nobody in particular, "I guess this is my lucky day. Bill, will you get a horse for me?"

Bill Earl rose and skirted the well to the stone corral where the horses were penned up.

"Can you get one for me, too, Sergeant?"

Noonan turned his head and looked at Thornton. "You aren't going anywhere, Mister. Just take it easy till I get back." He paused. "I want that white shirt you're wearing."

Thornton stared at him in amazement. "You want my shirt? What for?"

"Flag of truce," Noonan said curtly. "Me, I'm going to have a parley with the lieutenant. Now take it off."

Thornton had no choice but to do what he was

told. He stripped off his coat and shirt and gave the shirt to Noonan. His soft white flesh above his trousers and proper shoes was such a ridiculous sight that several of the men laughed.

When Earl brought a horse, Noonan mounted and said, "Hold him here," then turned his horse around and disappeared into the cut in the *malpais*. When he came to the sentry closest to the camp he said, "I'm going out to make talk with the lieutenant. Keep me covered. Don't shoot unless I do."

The sentry nodded and started down the road a few feet behind Noonan.

At the edge of the *malpais* Noonan put his horse down the road, and with his good hand waved Thornton's white shirt. When he judged he was just out of rifle range of the camp he halted and waited in the blazing morning sun. It was only a matter of minutes before Lieutenant Overman rode out to meet him, and now Brick drew his pistol and rested it on the leg. Overman approached and reined it. He, too, had a pistol in his hand.

"I take it you want to talk, Sergeant."

"You can drop the Sergeant, Lieutenant. I'm not in the Army. You didn't see my papers, did you?"

Lieutenant Overman only shook his head.

"So you're talking to a civilian," Noonan continued. "I'm here to make a deal with you."

"Deal?" Overman seemed puzzled. "Go ahead and talk."

"We've got Thornton. He walked into our camp and wanted to buy a horse. This is his shirt."

"Oh, I believe you, Noonan, but who is the 'we' you spoke of?"

Noonan grinned. "My boys that stopped you in the *malpais*."

Overman's thin brown face held a faint smile of irony. "One of your boys must not like you much, Noonan, if he'll shoot you in the back."

"I took care of him. That's why I left you, so I could get him."

Now Overman said coldly, "State your business, Noonan."

"I'll trade you back Thornton for the rifles."

"Rejected," Overman said promptly.

"Then I'll kill him."

"I believe that." There was a fathomless contempt in Overman's tone.

Noonan was puzzled by Overman's indifference to his threat. "I'll leave his body where we're talking now, so you can bury him."

Overman's face was impassive. "All right."

"You don't look like you cared a damn," Noonan observed.

"I'll regret his death, especially because it's unnecessary."

"That's what I'm trying to tell you," Noonan said. "It isn't necessary. Just give me the rifles in exchange for him."

Lieutenant Overman shook his head slowly. "Noonan, John Thornton walked away from the train by his own choice, knowing the danger involved. I'm not going to ransom him back with government property. He is a civilian and of age. The Army offered him protection and he refused it. It's that simple."

"Then if you want him dead, he's as good as dead now."

"That's up to you. But if you kill him you're more stupid than I think you are, Noonan. Since I refuse to accept your blackmail, Thornton's of no use to you at all. Sell him a horse and send him on his way."

"No, he's a dead man. Last chance, Lieutenant. Do you want him back or don't you?"

"Not on your terms, Noonan. That's all."

Noonan could not keep the anger out of his face and, seeing it, Lieutenant Overman could not resist a parting thrust. "I think you'd better leave now, Noonan. You leave first."

"Why don't you leave first?"

"Because if you're going back to butcher a man like a hog, you'd shoot me in the back if I left first. Now, on your way."

Cursing savagely, Noonan pulled his horse around and started back toward the *malpais*.

7

Overman waited a minute, then wheeled his horse and
rode back to camp. He dismounted by the ashes of the
campfire, handed his horse over to one of the troopers,
and went over to Juliana, who was sitting in the shade
of one of the wagons.

Lieutenant Overman was dripping with perspiration. He took off his hat; mopped his forehead with his
neckerchief, and sat down beside Juliana.

"The men said that was Sergeant Noonan you
were talking to," Juliana said.

"It was," Overman said grimly. "You were right—
Noonan deserted. Our polite sergeant is the leader of
this gang that's hounding us."

Juliana accepted this without surprise. "What did
he want?"

Overman said tonelessly, "He's got John Thornton.
He'll give us back Thornton alive if we give him the
rifles. If I won't, he'll give him back dead."

There was disgust and horror in Juliana's face,
then she said softly, "That's an impossible decision to
make, Dick."

"Not impossible at all," Overman said curtly. "I
refused him the rifles."

Juliana was silent for a full minute, her face pen-
sive and sad. Overman noticed she was crying silently,
making no sound, but the tears were there. "That means
he'll be killed, doesn't it?"

"I wonder," Overman said tiredly. "I pointed out
to Noonan that since I would not be blackmailed it was
stupid to kill Thornton." He clenched his fist and pound-
ed his knee for emphasis, as he said, "What good will it
do Noonan when it won't get him his rifles?"

"I know," Juliana said quietly, and then she

looked at Overman. "John has changed so since we started out. What made him?"

"I have my own idea. He lost his girl."

Juliana's lips parted in amazement. "You aren't talking about me. How could he lose me when he never had me?"

Overman smiled wryly. "He thought he did until Dave came along." He watched the blush come into Juliana's face.

"That's not true, Dick! Dave Harmon means nothing to me."

"I think he does. I know he means something to me. If we get out of this mess, we'll all owe him our lives. He means something to all of us, but in a special way for you, I think."

"I don't understand you," Juliana protested.

"Miss Juliana, you can hide it from yourself, but it's impossible to hide it from other people." Lieutenant Overman rose. "I've got to get on the job. I think we may be busy today." When Juliana only looked puzzled, the lieutenant continued, "I was trying to figure it out on the way back from talking with Noonan. Remember how Thornton came to despise us all? I'm sure he told Noonan about the additional men we're expecting, maybe tonight. I think Noonan might attack before Dave returns. I want to be ready."

He nodded good-bye and set out to round up his troopers.

The lieutenant's last words scarcely registered with Juliana. She was thinking of what Overman had said about herself and Dave Harmon. Was it true that her attention to Dave Harmon was the cause of the change in John? She enjoyed Dave's company and she admired him as much as Overman did, but wasn't that all?

She set herself to review her actions in the past few days. True, on the first night out she had talked with him and was almost rebuffed by him. True, she had sought him out at Layton's place, but wasn't it to defend John? True, she had queried him about his reasons for leaving the Army. It was also true, she had to admit, that most of her conversations with Lieu-

tenant Overman were about Dave Harmon. But was all
this more than just normal curiosity about a likeable
man with a somewhat mysterious past and present?
Had she really missed him in the few hours he had
been gone?

Honesty compelled her to answer yes. Since last
night when he left, she had experienced an abysmal
sense of fear. Lieutenant Overman was still what he had
always been, a brave, competent officer, but something,
some driving guidance and stubborn optimism of the
troopers and teamsters, was lacking. Had Dave Harmon been here, he would never have let John Thornton,
with his dangerous information, get out of camp. It
was as if all of them, Overman included, were in a state
of suspension waiting for Dave's return.

Dave and Solly Liston had pushed their *remuda*
steadily south during the relatively cool night hours. As
soon as there was light enough to see well, Dave
dropped back from his position at point to tell the
teamster, "I'm going to swing out and hunt sign of
Adams' tracks, Solly. Keep them at a walk and if you
hear me shoot, bring the herd to me. You might as
well eat while you ride, since we won't stop."

Solly, a taciturn, bearded old-timer, simply nodded,
and Dave swung southwest away from the horse herd.
He did not think they were far off Adams' course, and
he hoped to be able to pick up Adams' tracks. The
sandy marl of the desert floor around the base of the
barren Harquahalas was soft enough to hold the im-
print of a horse's shoe or a man's boot.

He rode slowly, scanning the desert floor for any
sign of Adams' passage. He judged it to be near a mile
when he came to the unmistakable sign of Adams'
bootprints pointing their stubborn way north. He pulled
out his pistol and fired, then holstered it, opened his
saddle bag, and ate his brief breakfast.

Idly he speculated on what he would find at the
water hole where Adams and the detail were stranded.
If the Apaches who had stolen the horses picked up
reinforcements, they were more than likely to return
and wipe out the detail. Chances were they would wait

until the detail's rations were eaten and they were forced to move. The Indians would reason that once the detail was away from water and afoot, they could be wiped out. It was difficult to tell always what motivated these Indians. Sometimes they seemed to raid only for the horses they could steal. Other times their sole motivation seemed to be to kill and torture. Invariably, though, they had to have superior numbers before they would attack.

Now Dave saw the *remuda* headed at an angle toward him and he put Noonan's horse into a slow walk. Presently the *remuda* caught up with him and fell in behind him.

This would be a punishing day for the horses, Dave knew, but there would be water at the end of it. All that morning he and Solly took a fresh mount from the *remuda* every hour, for the horses and mules were being driven at a fast pace in the blasting heat of the desert plains. By frequently changing to fresh mounts they spread the work over the whole *remuda*.

It was in late morning that Dave saw ahead of him black specks on the desert. Coming closer, he saw the specks were buzzards, and he knew they were feasting on what was left of Trooper Reardon's body. Swinging wide of it so as not to alarm the horses, Dave picked up the tracks again. Now there were two sets of footprints. Since Adams had said that the going was painfully slow with Reardon hurt and drunk, Dave knew they were within a few miles of the detail.

Two hours later Dave saw more dark shapes in the far distance, and as they came closer he saw the shapes move. Relief flooded him then, for surely the shapes were cavalry blue, which meant the Apaches had not returned.

When they rode into the camp the men cheered, some of them patting the horses as if they had never seen a horse before.

Dave swung out of the saddle to face Corporal Chasen, who said, "You make a mighty pretty sight, Mister. They made it to you, did they?"

"Only Trooper Adams," Dave said. "Reardon's dead on the desert. Where's your officer, Corporal?"

"Just a minute, sir, and I'll have my men water and grain the horses." He moved off toward his men and Dave looked at the desolate camp, at the lone tent, at the splintered wagon, at the propped-up blankets and, finally, at the two huge mounds of rock. Where, he wondered, was Lieutenant Miller?

Now Corporal Chasen came back and Dave sized him up. He looked a seasoned trooper, with that air of quiet authority that comes from long service and chevrons on the sleeve. His swarthy, broad face, with the startling blue eyes, was pleasantly homely. He halted in front of Dave. "You were asking about the Lieutenant, Mister—"

"Dave Harmon."

"—Harmon," Corporal Chasen finished. "He's dead, sir. Murdered."

"Apaches?"

"No, sir, by one of my men. I call them my men because I have the only rank and had to take command. I'd like you to see something, Mister Harmon, before I tell you any more. Will you come over to the tent?"

Dave followed him over to the low tent. Chasen reached into it and came up with Lieutenant Miller's notebook. "Will you read the last couple of pages, Mister Harmon? Just sit down in the shade."

Dave slacked into the shade of the tent and opened the notebook. Apparently these were entries which were intended to go in Lieutenant Miller's finished report. When he came to the entry of the day when lots were drawn, he already had some understanding of Miller's character, which was that of a martinet, but a painstakingly honest one.

When Miller's notes described how he wished to punish the two sentries who had allowed the Apaches to steal the horses, by sending them for help, Dave wondered at the man. As he read of Corporal Chasen's warning that he might be murdered if he ordered men into the desert instead of allowing them to draw lots, Dave nodded. *Chasen was right,* Dave thought. Then, with increasing interest, he read of Miller's decision to make work for his men by hauling rock from two miles away to wall up the water hole.

The last entry told of the men's discontent, their exhaustion and their hatred of him, and of his decision to put them unnecessarily on half-rations and to continue putting them to grinding and useless tasks.

The sum of the entries told Dave that Corporal Chasen was an excellent non-com serving under a cruelly misguided officer.

When he had closed the notebook, he rose and handed it to Chasen, and asked, "What's the ending, Corporal?"

"He was knifed in the back while he slept."

"Know who did it?"

Chasen smiled grimly. "I know the man who told me he did. He'll deny it, and since there were no witnesses, he'll go free."

"Where is he?"

"He's lying under the wagon with a broken jaw, sir."

Dave looked levelly at Corporal Chasen. "Accident, no doubt," Dave said drily.

"No, sir, I can't say it was," Chasen said. "Since a courtmartial will free him, I thought I'd get in ahead of it." Then he added. "It's only officers who can't hit an enlisted man, Mister Harmon, and I'm not an officer."

Dave smiled. "I hope you are some day, Corporal."

"Thank you, sir. Lieutenant Miller is buried on the rock bar he spoke of in his book."

"That's appropriate," Dave said. "Corporal, why don't we give the horses some rest before we start out? Better leave the wagon, don't you think? We'll be at our camp by midnight, I hope."

"Right, sir."

"Can your trooper with the broken jaw ride?"

"I'll see that he does."

"You might tell your men they'll start soldiering again when we hit camp." Dave then told Corporal Chasen the situation at the wagon train.

"Then we'll make the difference," Corporal Chasen said with pleasure. "That'll be a fair trade for you coming to us."

After the horses, fed and watered, were rested, the detachment saddled up. Dave identified Wilson by the handkerchief tied around his head to hold his jaw together. He was fat, sullen, and obviously shunned by his fellow troopers. Before the order to mount was given, Dave moved over to Corporal Chasen's side. "Is there ammunition in the wagon, Corporal?" he asked.

"Lots of it, sir."

"Maybe you'd better drop a trooper back to fire it when we're out of range. I'd hate to think the Apaches would stumble on it if we left it."

"I'll do it myself, sir."

Chasen quietly gave the order to mount and the detail set out without him. When they were half a mile distant, the ammunition began to go off. Soon after, Chasen caught up with them and they headed north, leaving a lifting pillar of smoke in the brassy sky behind them.

Now that they were headed back to camp, Dave wondered what the day had brought for Juliana and the others. It had probably been a day of watchfulness, of boredom, and searing heat, with no movement of riding or driving to give even a suggestion of a breeze. Thornton was probably still sulking or arguing, in his supercilious way, with Overman. Thornton had disapproved of this trip and would doubtless voice it again and again to Overman.

Dave speculated now on Juliana's feelings for John Thornton. At the beginning of the journey he had assumed that there was a romance between Juliana and Thornton. His protectiveness toward her and her defense of him had indicated to Dave that their feelings toward each other were more than just friendship. Yesterday, however, when Thornton had proposed giving the guns to the men who were after them, Juliana had sided with Lieutenant Overman. Obviously the man considered Juliana's stand a breach of their friendship, and he wondered if Juliana thought this, too.

Thornton, Dave thought, was an opinionated fool,

perhaps harmless enough in his own environment, but he did not belong in the West. He had the Eastern attitude toward the army of the West, which could be summed up in few words: it was officered by incompetents, its enlisted men were riffraff, it persecuted the Indians, and in every department, including battle, it failed expensively. Juliana knew better, and Dave shrewdly guessed that this might be at the bottom of their differences. He hoped there were real differences, because the thought of Juliana Frost married to John Thornton was intolerable. He made a sudden decision, in the middle of that heat-blasted desert, that he would risk offending her by telling her so.

When Brick Noonan returned to his camp at King's Wells his fury at Overman's refusal of his ultimatum was only slightly lessened. He wanted to think about his next move in private, but he wanted more to get out of this torturing sun. The only shade available had to be shared with his men and with Thornton.

Dismounting by the well in front of his men, he handed his horse over to Bill Earl and seated himself in the shade beside Thornton, who, in spite of the heat, had put on his coat to hide his naked torso. Noonan tossed Thornton his white shirt and while Thornton was putting it on Noonan regarded him.

Overman was right, he thought. It was stupid to kill the man when there was absolutely nothing to be gained by his death. Come to think of it, Thornton had given him information that was of value and must somehow be put to use.

Noonan said abruptly, "How much money are you carrying, Thornton?"

Thornton looked startled. "Why, in the neighborhood of three hundred dollars, I should judge."

"That's what your horse will cost you," Brick said pleasantly. He was hoping that Thornton would protest and haggle, which would give him a chance to turn him loose afoot. However, Thornton only nodded agreement. "That includes food and a saddle, doesn't it, Sergeant?"

"It includes food, but no saddle. We've got no extras." This was a lie, for he had the saddle from Bailey's mule.

"Does it include information, too?"

"As much as we're able to give you."

"Then where's the next water?"

Noonan lied blandly, "I'm a stranger to these parts, Mister Thornton, but I'll ask the boys." He turned to his men and, because his back was to Thornton, he could wink. "Any of you know where the next water is?" Very likely half of the men present knew, but they only shook their heads, muttered they were new here too, or else said no.

Noonan turned back to Thornton. "Just keep on the road till you come to Camp Date. I've heard it's ahead."

Noonan waited for Thornton to request a gun, too. But Thornton only got up, reached in his coat pocket for his wallet, and emptied its entire contents of gold eagles into Noonan's outstretched hand.

"Now, may I have my horse, please?"

Noonan pocketed the money and called to Earl, "Bill, give him one of the wagon mules. Put a hackamore on him."

"You said you'd sell me a horse," Thornton said.

"A mule's better in this country," Noonan replied easily. "Besides, we can't spare a horse."

Presently Bill Earl led a mule out of the stone corral. He fashioned a hackamore in place of bridle and bit, then led the mule to the walled-off section of the spring used for stock watering. That reminded Thornton that he must fill his canteen to the brim. He walked over under the amused gaze of the loafing men and topped off his canteen.

When Bill Earl led the mule out and handed the rope to Thornton, Noonan sat up and watched.

"Want a leg up?" Bill Earl asked.

Thornton nodded, and Bill cupped his hands to serve as a step for Thornton.

No sooner had Thornton hit the mule's back and Bill Earl had ducked away from the mule than it began to buck and pitch. In a matter of seconds Thornton had slid over the mule's neck into the sand.

His fall brought the expected laughter from the men. Bill went over, caught the mule's rope, and led it back to Thornton, who had scrambled to his feet and replaced his hat. His face was not only flushed with heat, but with embarrassment.

"Maybe you'd better get me a more gentle animal," Thornton said.

Brick Noonan called, "All of 'em are only harness broke, Thornton. Just stick with it."

Resignedly Thornton accepted another leg up, and the mule came uncorked again. This time Thornton stuck with it a little longer before he was thrown. Again, there was the cruel laughter from Noonan's watching men.

Now, for the first time, Thornton knew both anger and fear. How was he going to handle this beast by himself when he could neither mount it alone, nor stay when he was on it? Beyond that, was he even going to get out of camp?

He looked at Noonan and his men, hating them for their derisive laughter and for the obvious pleasure they were getting out of his troubles. Still, there was only one thing to do, and Thornton, although never an expert horseman, knew it had to be done. He tried again, and was thrown, he tried once more, stayed on a little longer, and was thrown again. On his fifth try, battered and bruised, he succeeded in staying aboard the now tired mule, which had exhausted itself with its exertions in the blazing heat.

Noonan came forward then with a saddle bag stuffed with bacon and bread. He handed up the canteen and saddle bag to the shaking and panting Thornton.

"There you are, Mister Thornton. Have a good ride."

"Thank you," Thornton said stiffly. He drummed his heels into the mule's side, but it did not move. Bill Earl came up, kicked the mule in the belly, and only then did the animal grunt and get into motion past the adobe and down the road.

John Thornton's plans of this morning had worked out almost exactly as intended. He had escaped camp, he had bought a mount of sorts, he had food and water, and he was out of this distasteful and dangerous quarrel between people he cared nothing about. Yet somehow the reality did not match the expectation. He was exhausted, afraid of his mount, and suddenly he was terribly alone in this cruel, unfamiliar land bordered on two horizons by distant and hostile mountains.

As the day wore on into mid-afternoon, the mule resignedly plodded on at a gait it chose itself. When Thornton passed a few rocks that could offer shade, he was afraid to dismount for fear the mule would bolt back to camp. His legs ached miserably and he could find no comfortable seat on the mule's bare back. His few attempts to spur the animal, rein him in, or guide him, had failed. He was simply aboard a beast that had pulled a wagon over so many miles of road that it had learned to travel stubbornly.

The farther he rode that afternoon, the greater his loneliness became. What had been the constant irritations in camp now seemed trivial in the light of his present solitude. There was talk there, however bad, and companionship, however boring, and there was shade, blessed shade. He wondered, his alarm growing hourly, when he would come to the next water. He knew that he should pause to rest and water his mule, but some deep pessimism told him that he could not stop the mule, and that even if he did, the mule would very likely turn around and head back for camp.

It was late afternoon when Thornton knew that he could not go much farther without resting. If only he could find, in all this flat desert, some shade where he could tie his mule and lie down and sleep for an hour. With rest, and by splitting his remaining water with his mule, maybe both he and his mount would have strength enough to ride on until they came to water.

Far ahead of him he could see a gentle rise in the flat desert, and he hoped wildly that somewhere on its far side there would be a patch of shade where he could dismount. As he approached the rise he saw that the road swung gently to the right to avoid a rough promontory of rock. On the other side perhaps there would be a bank that would give him some shade. As he began to round the low promontory, only some ten feet high, his mule's ears pricked up alertly. Was there water ahead? Thornton, weary as he was, didn't think so, for the mule's pace slackened and he snorted in short, sharp breaths. If there were water ahead, the mule's pace would have increased, he knew.

The mule stopped then and Thornton could feel the animal trembling under him. He did not know if it was from fear of something unseen behind the smooth rock or from weariness, but he did know that he could not sit here listening to his own heart pound and feeling the mule's heart pumping against his legs. He kicked savagely at the mule's flanks, but the animal would move only sideways, not ahead; its attention was riveted on what lay on the other side of the smoooth rock. Whatever it was, John Thornton realized now, for the first time, that there was nothing he could do about it, since he had neglected to bring a gun from camp, or to buy one from Noonan.

Suddenly the mule seemed to make up its mind. It gave a vast snort, wheeled, and started to trot back in the direction from which it had come. Vainly Thornton tried to turn it, but he had not the strength. He was so concentrated on trying to master his mule that only belatedly did he hear the sound of hoofbeats.

He turned and saw four mounted Apaches, their ponies at a dead run in pursuit. He had time only to count them and to note their red headbands before he turned and tried with his rope to whip his exhausted mule into greater speed.

The rest was only a matter of moments. John Thornton's mind was to register only the twang of a bow before the arrow hurtled into his back, slamming the breath out of him and replacing it with an agony of pain. With mute astonishment, even denial that it existed, he saw a foot of arrow sticking out of his chest

ahead of him, but that was only an instant before he
swayed off his mule to crash onto the desert floor and to
die within seconds.

Well before noonday Lieutenant Overman had his
camp prepared. The ring of wagons had been closed
tighter. His men had managed to clear enough cargo in
each high-sided wagon to allow space for a man inside.
Among the tools which were part of the freight to
Whipple, Overman had found augers with which he
had bored holes in the wagon sides at the height where
a kneeling man inside could poke through a rifle and
sight in it. All available guns were counted and loaded,
and placed inside the wagons along with extra ammunition. It turned out that each man had two repeating rifles plus side arms.

When the extra rifles were stowed inside the wagons, Lieutenant Overman assigned the best marksman
and a loader for him to each wagon. That done, he ordered each wagon crew to stay in the shade of its
assigned wagon so that they could climb inside in a matter of seconds in case of alarm. For Lieutenant Overman was convinced that Noonan, rather than wait for
an extra nine men to fight him, would try to over-
power the wagons before reinforcements arrived.

Juliana watched troopers and teamsters as they finished their tasks, and she shared with them the simple
noon meal which she had prepared. There were no
longer two fires; the imminent danger of attack had
drawn teamsters, troopers, and their officer into one
close group.

Afterwards, when the men had scattered to their
places, Overman sank down in the shade of the tarp he
had hung from the side of the wagon and propped up
with new shiny yellow shovel handles which had been
found among the freight. Juliana, her dress clinging to
her body in this oven heat, was already seated on one
of the blankets under it.

"I think we're ready for them," Overman said.
"You know you're my loader for this wagon."

Juliana nodded absently, and after a moment's silence she asked with seeming irrelevance, "Dick, sup-

pose Dave brings in these nine more men, with them and with all the men we've got, do you think we could fight our way through the *malpais* to water?"

Lieutenant Overman's glance shifted away from her. He had been asking himself that question all morning and could not answer it with an optimistic affirmative.

Juliana went on, "If we can't fight our way through, then we'll have nine more men to supply with water."

"We'll make it through," Overman said, with confidence he did not feel. "When you have to do something, you do it."

Even before sundown Dave had rejected the notion of stopping to eat. He had set a pace during the blazing afternoon that was calculated to save the trail-weary animals. But now that the sun was down, he increased the pace. He wanted to be in camp well before moonrise. If he arrived after moonrise, the plan he had been turning over in his mind all afternoon would have far less chances of success.

The handle of the Big Dipper, his only clock, told him that it was close to ten o'clock when Corporal Chasen, riding beside him, said, "Look off to the right on the horizon, sir. If that's a star, it shines pretty steady."

Dave picked up the light, watched it a minute, then said, "I think that's our camp, Corporal."

The column now altered its course, and within half an hour they made out the bulk of the wagon train and its lanterns. Soon they were challenged by a sentry and passed and then Dave said, "Corporal, I wonder if you could halt your men on the east side of the camp with the wagons between you and the *malpais*. I'll bring lanterns over for unsaddling."

"If you want it that way, sir," Corporal Chasen said, in a tone of mystification.

Dave split off from the detail and headed for the lanterns where both Juliana and Overman, surrounded by troopers and teamsters, were waiting.

Dave rode in and swung out of the saddle as Overman said, in a puzzled voice, "Bring them over to the light, Dave. I'd like to look at them."

Now Chasen's order for dismount came clearly from the other side of the camp.

Dave said, "String along with me, Dick. Can you have your men take a couple of lanterns around there? I'll explain why later."

Bewildered, Lieutenant Overman gave the order to his men, who were already moving toward the newly arrived detail. Dave tied his reins to a wagon wheel and said, "I think we'd all better give them a welcome. You, too, Miss Juliana." In the dim light of the lanterns they walked around the wagon train and approached the dismounted detail. Juliana said to Dave, "Are they all right?"

"Mostly," Dave said. "You'll hear about it later."

"John's gone," Juliana said then. "He deserted us this morning."

Dave looked obliquely at her in the dim light to see what her face contained. It was certainly not grief, only a weary sadness.

"Dick will tell you about that," she added.

The lantern light picked out Lieutenant Miller's detail and they heard Lieutenant Overman, a few steps ahead of them, say, "Welcome, troopers. We'll feed you shortly." There was a pause. "Where's your officer?"

By that time Dave and Juliana had reached Overman's side. And now Dave called, "Corporal, would you come here, please?"

Out of the group of unshaven and dusty men, still holding their horses' reins, Corporal Chasen stepped out. He came up to them, halted, and saluted Overman. "Corporal Chasen reporting, sir."

By this time Trooper Adams had rejoined his old group, and they were shaking his hand and patting him on the back. To a man, they were aware that but for his stubborn determination and endurance they all would have died in the desert.

"Dick, I think you'll want to talk to Corporal Chasen in private," Dave said. He glanced at Chasen. "Have you Lieutenant Miller's diary, Corporal? I think you might tell the lieutenant your story like you told it to me."

"I've got it, sir," Chasen said. He reached into his hip pocket and drew forth the notebook, which he handed to the puzzled Overman. Overman took a lantern and said, "Come along, Corporal," and moved out of earshot, first ordering his men to build a fire and start preparing food for the newcomers.

It was an unnecessary order, for the troopers had already kindled the fire and were rustling grub. Dave noticed that Trooper Wilson was sitting off by himself in the dejected attitude of a pariah. On the faces of the other troopers, gaunt and unshaven as they were, there was an excitement of being here that they did not even try to hide.

"You'll want some food yourself," Juliana said. "We've got beans and bacon back at the other fire."

Dave nodded, and together they started around the wagons. Now Dave said, "Tell me more about Thornton."

"There's nothing much to tell," Juliana said. "One of your teamsters was sentry. John said he wanted to go over and look at the *malpais* and your man warned him to stay away from the road. When he got to the *malpais* he headed for the road, and that was the last any of us saw of him. Noonan saw him, though."

"Noonan's back then?" Dave said.

"Our Sergeant Noonan wasn't a sergeant, Dave. It's his gang that's fighting us."

As Juliana prepared the meal she told Dave of Noonan's offer to trade Thornton for the rifles, and of Overman's refusal. Nobody knew Thornton's fate, but Overman was certain that Thornton had told Noonan of Dave's journey for reinforcements and had prepared the wagons for a raid that had never come off.

Dave listened carefully, thinking that Overman had been right both in his decision to refuse the blackmail and to fortify the camp in the best fashion he could.

Juliana gave Dave his food and he wolfed it hungrily; she seated herself beside him and began to speculate on Thornton's fate.

"I wonder what possessed John to leave?" she said musingly. "Surely Noonan didn't influence him to desert and join his gang. John's not that kind."

"No, he's not," Dave said slowly. "But what kind is he?"

Juliana looked at him in puzzlement. "Why, he's selfish, for one thing, or he would never have deserted us. He's vain and stubborn and I'm afraid he's more than a little foolish." She paused, lost in thought for a moment. "On shipboard he was thoughtful and pleasant. He was the best company a person could have, but when he got into this desert something happened that I don't understand. He was so sure he knew everything, and he really knew nothing."

That sums him up, Dave thought with relief. No woman about to marry a man would admit these flaws in his character.

"Now I'll confess something," Dave said. "I thought you and Thornton were close to being engaged or married."

Juliana blushed, but her voice was steady as she said, "Never. I want more in a man than entertainment."

Dave frowned, and, as always, the act made his eyepatch slip a little. He placed a finger to it and shoved it back into position, while Juliana watched him.

"I don't reckon you saw him under the best of conditions," he said.

"I saw him under the worst. So I know him. Dick didn't desert us. You didn't desert us. That's the difference."

They were interrupted by the approach of Lieutenant Overman, who sat down on the blanket beside them and crossed his booted legs. Taking off his hat, he laid it slowly, almost thoughtfully, on the blanket. "That's quite a man, that Corporal Chasen," Overman said. "And Lieutenant Miller, in his own way, was quite a man, too."

At Juliana's look of polite puzzlement Overman told her of the story contained in Lieutenant Miller's notebook and of his murder. He ended by saying reluctantly, "If I were a proper officer I'd probably put the whole detail under arrest to be held for court-martial."

Dave smiled. "But you're not a proper officer, are you, Dick?"

A look of pleasure touched Overman's lean face. "I am not, or I wouldn't have shaken hands with Corporal Chasen for breaking Trooper Wilson's jaw." Then the look of pleasure faded from Overman's face. "Can you tell me now why you wanted Miller's troopers on the other side of the camp?"

"That's a question I'll have to answer with a question." Dave paused. "How do you propose to use the additional troopers that came in with me? You were into the *malpais* and I've been through it lots of times. Do you think you could storm it, or do you think there's a chance of pairing off your men to hunt down each member of Noonan's gang?"

Overman thought a moment. "I don't think it could be stormed. Even with twice the number of men we've got, it would be impossible."

"Do you think they could be hunted down individually?"

"I don't like it, but I think that's our only hope. We would have to send some sort of decoy through the cut to draw their fire so we could spot the location of the riflemen. Even then, once they were located my men would be sitting ducks, when they expose themselves to get a rifleman." He shook his head. "It'll be bloody, but I don't see any other way."

"What if you could draw them out of the *malpais?*" Dave said quietly.

Overman scowled. "Why should they come out? They're keeping us from water, and that's what they want." He paused. "Incidentally, the additional troopers and their mounts that you brought in have cleaned us out of water. So we've got to fight through."

"But what if you could draw them out of the *malpais?*" Dave persisted.

"We'd take them."

Now Dave rose and moved away from the lantern light out into the darkness.

Juliana looked questioningly at Lieutenant Overman. "What's he after, Dick?"

"Blessed if I know," Overman answered in a puzzled voice.

Presently Dave came back and sank down on the blanket again. "Dick, I figure we have more than a half-hour before moonrise." At Overman's nod, Dave went on slowly, "That's why I asked Corporal Chasen to camp where the wagons would screen them from the *malpais*. Surely one of Noonan's gang is watching us from the *malpais*. I doubt if they have a telescope, but even if they have, I don't think they know that Miller's men are here."

Overman shook his head and grinned swiftly. "Dave, you're trying to tell me something, but you're afraid you'll hurt my feelings. Man, go ahead and say it."

It was Dave's turn to smile. "Thanks. All right, I'm suggesting this. They don't know that Miller's men are here. Suppose that in a few minutes we start to form up the train to head back for Layton's Wells. It would indicate to Noonan, who knows our water situation, that we're leaving to head back. If they do have a telescope and they've seen me, so much the better. It would look to them as if I returned without finding Miller's detail, wouldn't it?"

Overman was so intent on Dave's words that he barely nodded, and Dave continued. "Once the sentry sees the train forming up he'll go back and tell Noonan, won't he?"

"As fast as he could ride, I'd think," Overman said.

"Then while the sentry's gone and before the moon rises you could put every one of your troopers into the *malpais*. When Noonan gets the word the train is forming I think he'll wait for moonrise and then strike. By moonlight a strung-out train would offer an easy target, and Noonan would figure that we'd have to corral again to protect ourselves. Maybe he won't wait to attack until we form up. At all costs he can't let us move far, because once our water's gone he'll figure we'll surrender the guns for passage to the Wells."

He paused a moment and then went on. "When he comes through, we ambush him."

Before Dave finished speaking the excitement had come into Overman's face. Now he slapped his knee. "That's it!" he cried. "That's it!" He leaped to his feet and ran around the circle of wagons. In moments the camp was boiling with activity, and more lanterns were lighted. Both teamsters and troopers fell into furious action, manhandling the wagons clear so the harness teams could be hooked up.

8

Dave watched a moment and then said to Juliana, who had been silent, "I'd better tell Bailey and Everts what's happening."

He started to rise, but Juliana put a hand on his arm. "Dave, you're a kind man really. Did anyone ever tell you?"

"Nobody ever had a reason to," Dave said, almost gruffly.

Juliana smiled. "Dick has, so I'll say it for him."

"We're not out of this yet," Dave said. "If we get out of it, it'll be thanks to Dick and his troopers."

"Who invariably do what you gently suggest, Dave."

In embarrassment Dave rose, and turned and headed for the supply wagon where Everts and Bailey had been yarning with the troopers. It was here that Lieutenant Overman found him and drew him aside. "Dave, my detail will take the north side of the road. I wish you'd lead a detail to cover the south side."

"A one-eyed man isn't supposed to see well at night," Dave said, drily.

"I know one who will, all right. Will you take the detail?"

"Sure," Dave said.

"I've put Wilson to helping your teamsters. I guess

it doesn't matter how fast we get hooked up, just so it looks as if we're moving."

Dave nodded assent.

On the far side of the corralled wagons Corporal Chasen and his men were readying themselves for the foray. The case of ammunition had been broken out and the men were clustered around it as Corporal Chasen doled it out. Trooper Adams waited till the last man was supplied and then he limped up to Chasen. He was wearing a pair of borrowed boots too big for him, which made him look faintly ridiculous. When Chasen looked up and saw this slight, almost wizened figure, he smiled.

"I thought the lieutenant told you to stay off your feet, Adams."

Adams, too, smiled, which was a rare thing for him. "Corporal, I got a favor to ask."

"Go ahead and ask it."

"I want to go along."

Corporal Chasen frowned, then said in a kindly voice, "We got enough men, Johnny. Besides, I reckon you've earned a rest."

"No, I want to go along," Adams said stubbornly. "I belong with you."

Corporal Chasen rose, took off his hat, and scratched his head, dilemma plain on his face. "Orders are orders, Johnny, but I'll ask the lieutenant."

"Make it good, because I want to go along," Adams said.

Chasen hunted out Lieutenant Overman, who was talking with Juliana and Dave. They stopped talking when he approached, and Corporal Chasen said, "May I talk with the Lieutenant, sir?"

"Of course you can, Chasen. What's on your mind?"

"Sir, Trooper Adams wants to go with us. He says he can walk and he says he belongs with the detail."

Lieutenant Overman didn't answer immediately, while he weighed the request. Then he said, "What would you do, Corporal? Give him permission?"

"Yes, sir," Chasen said emphatically. "He's changed, sir."

Overman frowned. "Changed how, Corporal?"

"Well, sir, he was never much of a trooper before this. He'd dog a job when he couldn't duck it. None of the men liked him, and he didn't like them. He wasn't a troublemaker, he was just nothing."

"You think that long hike changed him?"

"Yes, sir, I do. We were counting on him, and he came through. He saved our lives, I reckon, and all of us know it. He—well, he amounts to something now, Lieutenant, and he knows it."

"Then take him along, by all means," Overman said.

Corporal Chasen hesitated before he blurted out, "May I ask the Lieutenant something else?" At Overman's nod he said, "What will they do to Adams for shooting Reardon?"

Lieutenant Overman answered promptly. "As far as I'm concerned, Trooper Reardon simply died in the desert from a sunstroke, brought on by excessive drinking. I intend to write in my report to Major North that Trooper Adams carried out his mission under conditions of extreme hardship and that I would be proud to have him serve under me. Does that answer your question, Corporal?"

Corporal Chasen almost smiled. "Yes, *sir*."

"Then get your men ready, Corporal. Harmon will go with you."

Shortly afterwards the two details headed out for the *malpais* afoot, with orders to walk cautiously and not to carry sabers, which they had already removed anyway. The two details skirted the breaking camp and converged noiselessly on the road where it entered the *malpais*. It was pitch-black in this wedge where the road lay, and Dave knew they were running the risk of bumping into a second sentry. However, he doubted if Noonan would think that two were necessary; only a watcher was needed to keep an eye on the camped train.

As they moved deeper into the *malpais* the moon began to come up. And now Lieutenant Overman began to spot his men and Dave's where the moonlight touched a straight stretch of the twisting road. Overman was careful not to scatter the men too widely or place them too far from the road. Dave knew that Overman could not count too heavily on the visibility by moonlight and that he wanted his men close and reasonably concentrated.

To each man Overman gave orders not to fire until he fired. The reason was obvious: he wanted the whole gang in the trap before the jaws closed. A jittery trooper at the far end who fired at sight could ruin the whole plan, and he impressed this on each man.

Dave took a place nearest the camp and carefully climbed up into the still warm *malpais*. The edges of the rock were razor-sharp and it was difficult to find a hand hold without cutting his palms. When he was some feet above the road he sat down on a rock which gave him clear sight of it in the growing moonlight.

Only now, in this utter stillness, did Dave have the chance to reflect on everything Juliana had told him since he returned to camp. He was not surprised that Thornton had deserted, but he wondered how Thornton proposed to continue his journey. It really didn't matter, Dave thought. What mattered was that Juliana didn't love him and that his conduct these last few days had wrecked any friendship between them. He suspected that Thornton's proposal to give Noonan's gang the rifles had opened the breach and that his desertion had widened it irrevocably.

Dave was aware, too, that Juliana liked him, and he wondered again if it was possible for an attractive girl to love a man with only one good eye. He had seen army wives accept with stoicism the physical mutilations their husbands had suffered in battle. These disfiguring wounds seemed in no way to change their loyalty and love for their men. That was understandable, Dave thought, because they had known and loved their whole men, and were bound to them by marriage vows if nothing else. But would any of them, meeting such a mutilated man for the first time, have chosen him? It was true that women married men not for their physical perfection, but for the intangible values of the spirit, for their goodness, for their honesty, and for their kindness. Many an ugly woman had these same virtues, but would a man, given the choice of a pretty woman with these same virtues and an ugly one, choose the homely one? He didn't think so.

His thoughts were interrupted by the distant faint sound of the clatter of shod hooves on rock. The plan was working then, Dave thought, unless this was a rare immigrant train traveling in the relative coolness of the night. He listened carefully as the sound increased in volume, and he noted the lack of the telltale jolting of wagon wheels on rock. No, these were mounted men, and soon they would know if it was Noonan's bunch.

Moments later, rounding the bend, the horsemen came in sight, riding two abreast in the moonlight. One of the first pair was Sergeant Noonan, his arm still in his trooper's neckerchief sling. The sight of him sparked a slow wrath in Dave, and he thought: *If he gets to me, he's mine.* Noonan was willing to sacrifice more than a dozen people to gain rifles to sell. The Apaches, Dave thought, at least had a reason for killing the men who were invading their homeland. Noonan had no reason at all save greed.

As the double line of horsemen came on, Dave counted thirteen men. Now they were roughly in the center of the area where Overman had spotted his men. Dave raised his rifle and waited impatiently for Overman's shot.

When the shot came, it was followed by a roar of gunfire erupting into the night. Dave spent a maddening two seconds trying to find his front sight and, not finding it, still fired at Noonan. As he levered in his second shell, he saw the wild tangle of milling horses, some with empty saddles, as the fusillade from the rocks continued. A riderless horse broke into a gallop below him, and now Dave saw that Noonan, still in the saddle, was going to try to break through.

This time Dave took no chances. He aimed at Noonan's horse and fired, and the horse's knees buckled and it plunged to earth. Noonan went flying over the horse's head, landed on his side, rolled over, and raced for the rocks all in one fluid motion. Again Dave shot, and again he knew he had missed.

Another riderless horse passed, and now Dave, in

a cold rage at his own ineptness, discarded his rifle, drew his pistol, and clambered down the rocks. He raced across the road, skirting Noonan's downed horse, and was almost run down by a horse whose rider had both arms wrapped around his belly and who was howling with pain.

Dave achieved the *malpais* on the far side of the road and began to climb. Noonan, he reckoned, could not go far with his wounded shoulder, which very likely had been reinjured in his fall. Holstering his pistol, Dave concentrated on climbing. He ignored the sharp, cutting edges of the *malpais* and plunged up the slope.

The withering rifle fire was still hammering behind him as he climbed. He labored up the slope until he was gagging for breath, and then he rested a moment, looking down at the scene of carnage.

Men's bodies were scattered on the road and two horses were down. One of the prone figures was firing up the slope and half a dozen rifles were searching him out. The rest of the troopers had ceased fire for lack of a target. Now Dave looked to the east into the upended *malpais*. He was sure that he had climbed higher than Noonan, and that Noonan was to the east and below him, probably hiding.

Slowly, then, Dave bent over and started his slow, silent way across the *malpais,* angling downward and in the direction of the camp. The firing had ceased now, and Dave heard the excited shouts of the troopers below. He quietly pushed on, and then below and ahead of him he heard a rock fall. He quickly sank behind a chunk of *malpais* and listened. The sound grew closer, and accompanying it was the sound of boots scraping on the *malpais*.

Abruptly, then, a figure appeared some thirty feet ahead of him between several low chunks of *malpais*. Noonan was bent over and Dave heard his great sobbing heaves as he fought for breath. Then Dave rose and stepped from behind his rock, gun in hand.

"Stop right there, Noonan!" he ordered flatly.

Noonan straightened abruptly and in a panic of haste raised his gun and fired blindly. It was way wide of Dave, and now Dave's own gun was lifted. He sighted briefly, the moon glinting on the gunbarrel, before he fired.

A great roaring sigh escaped Noonan as he fell backwards downhill and was hidden in the *malpais*.

Gun ready, Dave cautiously climbed down. He knew that he had hit Noonan, but he also knew that if there was a spark of life left in the man he would still fight. But when he saw Noonan's body from a distance of some ten feet, it did not stir. Dave moved down to it and knelt beside it. He could see by the moonlight that his slug had caught Noonan full in the chest, and Dave guessed that he was dead before he hit the earth.

Twelve of the thirteen men that comprised Noonan's gang were killed in the ambush, and Lieutenant Overman ordered the bodies laid in a ravine in the *malpais*. The burial detail would cover them with rock in the morning. Once that grim chore was done and the two dead horses dragged off the road, the troopers and Dave headed back for camp in the moonlight.

Waiting for them were Juliana and the remaining four teamsters who had managed to round up, with little difficulty, the outlaws' ten horses. As the weary detail tramped up to them Overman said, "Well, Miss Juliana, it's over. We go through to the Wells tonight."

"Are they——did they——" Juliana began.

"One got away," Overman said shortly. "I don't think he'll bother us." Then he raised his voice, "All right, men! Help Harmon's men hook up. We're moving to water tonight. How many of you were teamsters before you joined up?"

Half a dozen men in the circle around Overman spoke up and, pointing, Overman said, "You and you will each take one of Harmon's wagons. All right, let's go to work." As the troopers and teamsters scattered to their chore of harnessing the remaining mules, Dave saw that there were more than enough hands for the work and that his were not needed.

Now Overman turned to Juliana. "Miss Juliana, I'll put a trooper to driving your ambulance."

"I can drive it," Juliana said. "It's clear moon-light."

"Sorry, but you'll obey orders," Lieutenant Over-man said, and then smiled to take the bite off his words.

Dave said mildly, "I heard Corporal Chasen speak up when you called for teamsters, Dick. If you'll assign him my wagon, I'll drive the ambulance."

"I'll do that," Overman said cheerfully, and moved off to hunt down Chasen.

"All of a sudden I'm too delicate to drive the team, is that it?" There was a gentle humor in Juliana's tone.

"No, Dick's right," Dave said slowly. "There's the smell of death along that road and we may have trouble getting our teams past it."

Juliana nodded understandingly, and then she asked soberly, "Dave, it wasn't Sergeant Noonan who escaped, was it?" When Dave shook his head, she said, "I think I'm glad he didn't. I don't see how such a man could live with his conscience after tonight. It was Noonan who killed those men, not the troopers."

"I doubt if he had a conscience to live with," Dave said grimly. Then, to change the subject, he asked, "How are my two shot-up teamsters doing?"

"I talked with them just before you came back. They're thirsty, but then I guess all of us are, especially the animals."

One by one, as the wagons were hooked up, they were formed in a line. Overman, who had been assign-ing the outlaws' horses to Lieutenant Miller's detail, joined them now. "I think we're almost ready, Dave. Oh, I'm putting a dismounted trooper at the head of each lead team when we go through that stretch. We'll go through one at a time, so if you have to wait, that's why."

Dave nodded, and he and Juliana strolled over to the ambulance whose teams were hitched up and wait-ing. As they passed the troopers, who were exchanging their own saddles for the outlaws' saddles, the men smiled at them. Even sober Trooper Adams smiled. In spite of this night's grim business, Dave knew that each of them hugged to himself the knowledge that he had been reprieved from death once more.

Dave handed Juliana up into the ambulance and unwound the reins as Lieutenant Overman formed up and mounted his escort. Slowly then the troopers and wagons got under way, headed for the cut in the *malpais*.

The smell of blood at the site of the ambush made the teams restive and uneasy, but Overman's plan to place a dismounted trooper at the head of each lead team worked well. None of the teams bolted and the passage was negotiated easily. If Juliana saw the dark stains in the sand and on the rocks, she did not comment.

Now the reaction of the weariness and the excitements of the day seemed to affect them both, and they were silent for a minute. Abruptly then Juliana asked, "Dave, have you ever thought of applying for a commission again?"

"Not really," Dave said slowly. "Not until this trip anyway."

"Mother wrote that the Army is desperately short of officers. The 'Benzine' board retired so many incompetent officers last year that there aren't enough good officers to go around. I know Dad would turn over heaven and earth to help you."

"There's this eye," Dave said drily. "I don't like it, and I don't think the Army would like it. And there's nothing to do about it."

"I like it," Juliana said simply.

Dave looked obliquely at her, in surprise. "Why do you?"

Juliana thought a moment, then she said slowly, "I can't exactly explain why. But that patch is sort of a badge that says nothing has got you licked."

"I know a lot of saloon riffraff that wear eye-patches," Dave said wryly.

"That's just it," Juliana countered. "You're not saloon riffraff full of self-pity. You're a good businessman and a better soldier. You proved that once, and I should think you'd like to prove it again."

Dave, his doubts resolved, put a hand out and took her small hand in his. "You've answered something for me, Juliana. Yes, I think I will try it again."

ABOUT THE AUTHOR

LUKE SHORT, whose real name was Frederick D. Glidden, was born in Illinois in 1907 and died in 1975. He wrote nearly fifty books about the West and was a winner of the special Western Heritage Trustee Award. Before devoting himself to writing westerns, he was a trapper in the Canadian Subarctic, worked as an assistant to an archeologist and was a newsman. Luke Short believed an author could write best about the places he knows most intimately, so he usually located his westerns on familiar ground. He lived with his wife in Aspen, Colorado.

LUKE SHORT
BEST-SELLING WESTERN WRITER

Luke Short's name on a book guarantees fast-action stories and colorful characters which mean slam-bang reading as in these Bantam editions: